THE GHOST IN THE COUNTY COURTHOUSE

A MYSTERY SEARCHERS BOOK

BARRY FORBES

THE GHOST IN THE COUNTY COURTHOUSE

A MYSTERY SEARCHERS BOOK

VOLUME 2

By
BARRY FORBES

BAKKEN
BOOKS

Published by Bakken Books
2022

SERIES PRAISE FOR BARRY FORBES

AMAZING BOOK! My daughter is in 6th grade and she is home-schooled, she really enjoyed reading this book. Highly recommend to middle schoolers. *Rubi Pizarro on Amazon*

I have three boys 11-15 and finding a book they all like is sometimes a challenge. This series is great! My 15-year-old said, "I actually like it better than Hardy Boys because it tells me currents laws about technology that I didn't know." My reluctant 13-year-old picked it up without any prodding and that's not an easy feat. *Shantelshomeschool on Instagram*

I stumbled across the author and his series on Instagram and had to order the first book! Fun characters, good storyline too, easy reading. Best for ages 11 and up. *AZmommy2011 on Amazon*

Virtues of kindness, leadership, compassion, responsibility, loyalty, courage, diligence, perseverance, loyalty and service are characterized throughout the book. *Lynn G. on Amazon*

Barry, he LOVED it! My son is almost 14 and enjoys reading but most books are historical fiction or non-fiction. He carried your book everywhere, reading in any spare moments. He can't wait for book 2 – I'm ordering today and book 3 for his birthday. *Ourlifeathome on Instagram*

Perfect series for our 7th grader! I'm thrilled to have come across this perfect series for my 13-year old son this summer. We purchased the entire set! They are easy, but captivating reads and he is enjoying them very much. *Amylcarney on Amazon*

DISCLAIMER

Prescott, the former capital of the Arizona Territory, is considered by many to be the state's crown jewel. Aside from this central Arizona locale, *The Mystery Searchers* series is a work of fiction. Names, characters, businesses, places, events, incidents, and other locales are either the products of the author's imagination or used in a fictitious manner. Any resemblance to actual persons, living or dead, or actual events is purely coincidental.

Read more at www.MysterySearchers.com

For Linda,
whose steadfast love and encouragement
made this series possible

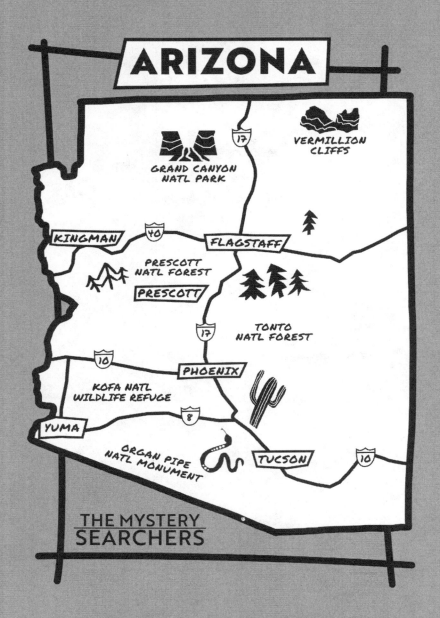

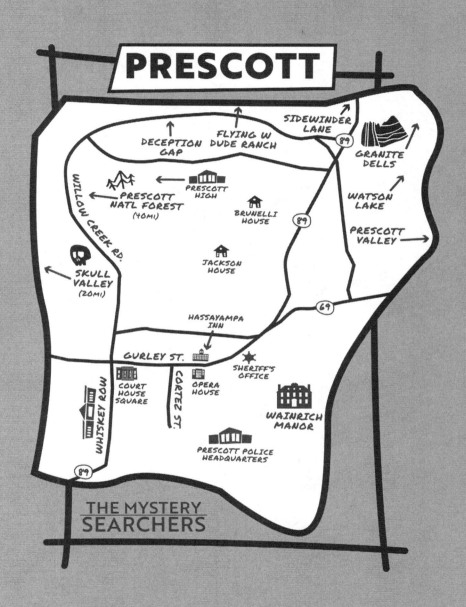

1

ALL FOR NOTHING

"**B**ut that's impossible, sir!" Tom blurted.

Sixteen-year-old twins Tom and Suzanne Jackson and their best friends, Pete and Kathy Brunelli, glanced at one another, baffled. They were sitting across a desk from Dr. William Wasson, the dean of Aztec College and the curator of the Yavapai Courthouse Museum. The dean had called them to an emergency Friday-morning meeting at the museum one hour before its opening to the public.

It was a fine day in early July. The Jacksons and Brunellis were fresh off their adventures on Apache Canyon Drive, a rural area just north of their mountain city home of Prescott, Arizona—"Everybody's hometown." Their success in foiling a cruel migrant-laborer smuggling and counterfeiting ring—and restoring a lost little girl from Mexico to her mother—was not only front-page news in *The Daily Pilot*, Prescott's hometown newspaper. The story had gone national. "Four young mystery searchers had solved the cases," it read. Local ones too.

The drama captured Dean Wasson from word one: "Mystery searchers." He repeated it later to his staff, "Just what we need."

The dean was a tall man in his sixties, distinguished-looking, with short gray hair and steel-rimmed glasses; he wore a white shirt and tie. Worry had etched his face. "Yes, you're right: it is impossible —or ought to be. Yet *someone* or *something* emerges at will and we're powerless to stop it." He shrugged his shoulders. "It's grotesque for sure. The museum staff calls it a ghost but we don't really believe that, of course. Then again, tell me what else walks through walls and bypasses the security system as if it doesn't exist!"

Kathy, official notetaker and the youngest member of the team, scribbled away at high speed, her eyes darting around the room.

"Is there a pattern to the ghost's appearances?" Pete asked. He was the impetuous one who always went straight to the point. "Like a particular day of the week?"

"Yes, and it's a strange one," the dean replied, peering at them over his glasses. "The ghost arrives *to the minute* —at two-oh-four a.m.—each time, but the nights are random. We haven't a clue if he'll show up tonight, sometime next week, or ever again, for that matter."

He paused, deep in thought. Seconds from a circular wall clock pierced the silence with a deadened sound.

"Hopefully, he—or she, or it—won't ever return, but we have our doubts. Our budget is tight—we're still in a fund-raising mode for all the renovations. No way can we afford to pay for a security guard here overnight, every night."

"Has anyone actually *seen* this ghost?" Suzanne asked, trying to wrap her mind around it.

"Oh, for certain!" Dean Wasson exclaimed. "The first time the mysterious thing appeared, it triggered the motion detectors. Strange, because there was no sign of a break-in. How would our system detect an immaterial entity? I've always wondered what the —well, whatever it is—was trying to tell us, because the alarm never activated again. We can't figure out why."

"When did this occur?" Tom asked. He was the quiet, thoughtful one. Every word counted.

"It was May twenty-second," the dean replied. "Roger Holloway, our custodian, received an emergency call from the security company. It was after two a.m. That call *should* have gone to our director, Gloria Waldner, but she was out on vacation. Roger lives just a few blocks away. He rushed over, arriving ahead of the police, and looked through the windows. A ghostly figure was moving through the displays. Shimmering white from head to toe. Scared poor Roger witless."

"Oh, wow, what happened next?" Kathy paused in her note taking. She shuddered. Could there be a ghost, after all? *Was it even possible?*

"The police arrived, but it was too late. The ghost was long gone." Dean Wasson lowered his voice. "At first, they didn't believe him, but I sure did. Roger doesn't make things up."

Kathy shook her head and sat up straighter. She continued to write, wide-eyed and alert.

"It didn't trigger the alarm after that first visit?" Pete asked.

"Never," the dean replied. "And since then the problem has only gotten worse. Much worse. Two priceless Hohokam relics—or artifacts, as we sometimes call them in archeology—disappeared one night just over a week later, on June third. They are—they were—the pride of our collection. That event threw us into a full-blown crisis."

"So at that point, the 'ghost' had visited twice and stolen two relics, both during its second appearance—but set off the alarm only the first time?" Tom asked.

"Correct."

"Then I'd say that whoever the thief is, he *wanted* the police—or someone on your staff—to see him during the first incursion. If the thief can disable or evade your security system, then he must have *wanted* you to see him in his ghost disguise."

"Maybe to distract you, even to make you panic," Pete said.

"Right," Suzanne added. Her confident style always impressed people. "He wasn't worried about getting caught, either."

"Quite so," Dean Wasson said, most impressed with their sober reasoning. "All of that sounds reasonable, and the detective assigned to the case said so too. But that still doesn't answer the burning question." He stood up and stared out the window toward Whiskey Row—Prescott's historic downtown street—with unseeing eyes.

"What's that, sir?" Kathy asked.

"How does it enter the museum?" the dean replied. A forefinger stabbed the air for emphasis. "How and *where*? Once lockdown occurs, no one gets in—or out. It's impossible."

"Are there any clues at all?" Suzanne asked.

"None." Dean Wasson turned back toward his visitors. "We've had multiple meetings with Prescott City Police officials in this office. They're as mystified as I am." The dean glanced over at the twins. "Your father is the chief of police."

"Yes, sir," Tom said. "He asked us to help in any way possible."

"We'll do everything we can," Suzanne said, trying to comfort the poor man. He appeared to be suffering from intense anxiety.

The dean smiled for the first time since his guests had arrived. "Please extend my thanks to your father. I know the department has worked hard on the case. They had a plain-clothes officer keep the place under covert surveillance every night for a week." He peered over his glasses. "Any idea what happened?"

"The Chief briefed us, sir," Suzanne replied. "The ghost failed to appear."

"Yes, correct again." The dean sat down, his chest visibly heaving. "Most disheartening—and a little suspicious. The detective in charge questioned us about the possibility of an inside job, of course. After all, my staff were the only ones who knew about the policeman. Who told the ghost?" He sighed again, louder this time, and sadder too.

"It's a bitter pill when one considers how we began," Dean Wasson continued. "The museum moved here—to the ground floor of the Yavapai County Courthouse—last fall. This majestic building is Prescott's finest, the jewel of the city, and a center of our cultural life. The cornerstone dates to 1916, well over a century ago. We're very proud of its history, but you know all that." The dean looked at the four best friends for confirmation. All born and raised in Prescott, they nodded.

"We played hide-and-seek on the courthouse steps when we were little," Kathy recalled, bringing a smile to everyone's faces. Those steps were part of Prescott's lore. Summer nights brought popular music festivals to Courthouse Plaza. Among the hundreds of people who crowded into the park, dozens found seating on the spacious stepped entrance to the famous old courthouse.

Dean Wasson stood up once more and paced his office floor. His gestures reflected the strained tone of his voice. "The location is perfect, much better than our previous quarters on campus. The museum has always been part of Aztec College, but we function quite independently. We have room to grow now. The structure—constructed from handsome granite quarried right here in Prescott—is a well-built architectural wonder. The design is even inspirational. Look at these windows." He pointed to one. "Plenty of natural light, which we filter to preserve our fragile textiles and so on. We raised the funds to install high-security windows and doors. And the museum boasts a fine alarm system." He exhaled audibly once more. "All for nothing. It has failed to protect our most valuable relics."

The dean paused, observing people as they strolled across the courthouse grounds. He cranked the window open. Birds sang from the dozens of American elm trees that ringed the building. Sounds of children laughing and playing in the surrounding four-acre park filtered into the office. The smell of fresh-cut grass wafted up around them. A mosquito settled on Tom's arm. He smacked it.

Once again, the dean turned toward them. He shook his head in disgust. "As I said, a month ago a major theft occurred. That was a terrible day. Everything seemed fine when we arrived at the museum that morning. But then—"

There was a sudden knock at the door.

2

THE ORB

"Oh, here she is now," the dean said, raising his voice. "Please come in, Gloria. I want you to meet these fine young people."

A trim, middle-aged woman, smiling and full of life, opened the door and rushed into the office. "Good morning, everyone!" Introductions followed.

"We're pleased to meet you, Mrs. Waldner," Suzanne said.

"The pleasure is all mine," she said, shaking hands and pulling over a chair. "Please call me Gloria. And congratulations on your Apache Canyon Drive adventure. That was *really* something."

Gloria, dressed in a tailored women's suit, appeared fashionable and elegant at the same time.

"Thank you," the young mystery hungers murmured. Gloria's warm, engaging personality lit up the room. They couldn't help but like her.

"I'm sorry to be late, William. We had a small emergency at home this morning."

"Nothing serious, I hope?"

"Oh, not at all. My oldest slept in." She laughed, winking at the four young detectives. "You know what that's like, right?"

"Not me," Kathy replied, "but my brother excels at it." Everyone chuckled as Pete rolled his eyes in mock annoyance.

Suzanne noted that the two administrators were on a first-name basis—quite normal for people who had worked together for years.

"Well, I was filling them in on the initial theft. Please take over," the dean said.

"Yes, that was quite a shock," Gloria said, picking up the thread of the conversation. "It's nerve-wracking because these relics are all one of a kind. From a historical perspective, they are irreplaceable."

"Thus, the great value of each one," Dean Wasson interjected.

"That morning," she continued, "I discovered that two rare Hohokam pots had disappeared. They came from an archaeological dig in northern Arizona. The museum accepted the donation in the nineteen-fifties as part of one of the founding bequests that initially built our collection. The artifacts were a thousand years old, the finest examples of Native American pottery in the state."

Pete sat up straight in his chair. "I'll bet they were worth a fortune."

"*Are* worth," Gloria corrected him. "Three hundred thousand dollars at auction, maybe more—much more. And to us, they're priceless. But that was only the beginning. Our collection included *four* Hohokam ceramics. Two weeks after the first theft, the second pair vanished. The total loss is close to six hundred thousand dollars in insurance terms."

It clearly pained the dean. "Humiliating, isn't it?" he said. "Imagine losing four priceless Hohokam artifacts!"

Tom whistled. "That's huge."

"It sure is," Dean Wasson said. His flat tone expressed a depressive state. "Those relics are a key to understanding our history. We are a custodian of Arizona's heritage, and this episode could be deadly to our reputation. It's heartbreaking. We're threatened by the decimation of the finest Hohokam collection in the world. I've never believed in ghosts, but how can you explain this?"

The room went silent for a few seconds.

"One question I have," Suzanne spoke up, "is why only *two* relics disappear at a time. Why not all of them?"

"We wondered that too," Gloria replied. "Prescott City Police provided two hypotheses. First, the thief can only carry two artifacts at a time. Why? Because they're very, very fragile and extreme care is necessary when handling them. Second—and this makes sense too—the police suspect that the thief is almost certainly selling the relics to a secret buyer or buyers first, *before* each theft."

"So it's like a shopping trip," the dean said ruefully. "First the thief sells the relics to an unscrupulous collector or dealer on the black market, *then* they disappear. He's stealing on spec, only when he has a buyer."

"At this stage, we're worried that the thieving ghost—or *what*ever or *whom*ever it is—will strike again," Gloria said. Lines of concern creased her forehead. "Personally, I believe it's only a matter of time."

Pete asked: "Well, the thief has already cleaned out the Hohokam exhibit. What else might be of interest?"

"We're concerned about the Sinagua exhibit," the dean said. "Petrified would be a better word. Our collection includes four Sinagua ceramics, all as precious as our Hohokam treasures—priceless, irreplaceable."

"The worst thing is, not only are we terrified of another theft," Gloria said, "but the police suggest that we *need* the thief to try again —and fail—if we are to have any chance of catching him... or her. They feel strongly that the thief's MO suggests local residence— someone who knows the museum and the town well."

"We alerted the FBI after the first theft," the dean added, "and they contacted Interpol. Both agencies monitor the illicit international art and antiquities market for items reported stolen. So far, no trace of our relics in that corner of the dark Web, or anywhere else."

"The chief of police, your father"—here he met first Suzanne's gaze, then Tom's—"doesn't want us to take any obvious new security precautions. 'Fool them into thinking they have a good chance of succeeding in another theft,' he said. 'We'll only catch them if they feel safe in coming back.' So one thing we're counting on is your absolute discretion."

"We can guarantee you that," Suzanne said. "Who has access to the museum?"

"We do," Dean Wasson replied, pointing to himself and Gloria. "Plus Roger Holloway, our custodian. Our assistant director, Jim Bright, does too. He's in Phoenix at the regional museum convention this week. Our other staff members are volunteer docents who lead tour groups, none with key access. The four of us on the permanent full-time paid staff have all served the college and this museum for the past fifteen years. I believe we are all above reproach—and beyond suspicion."

"Nobody could doubt that." Gloria's words seemed to reassure Dean Wasson.

"Only four keys exist in the world." The dean held one in his open hand. "And without one of these, there's no entry."

"What about the security company?" Suzanne asked. "Wouldn't they have a key?"

"Absolutely not," Gloria replied. "Way too many employees, which was a real concern. Plus, the system requires a five-digit passcode to open or lock the doors. We don't give that out, either."

"You mentioned cameras," Tom said.

"Yes, we have interior and exterior cameras," Dean Wasson replied. "Gloria will point them out to you later. We have downloaded the stills the cameras captured during each of the two thefts. Sure enough, it's there."

"*What's* there?" Suzanne asked.

"Well," Gloria said, "the inside camera captures still photos at ten-second intervals and stores them on the Cloud."

"Why not shoot continuous footage?" Tom asked, always curious about the technological aspects of any problem.

"Budget considerations," Dean Wasson replied. "Shooting only stills enables us to keep our security material for longer and at much lower cost than video footage, which requires vastly more

Cloud storage space. Remember, the cameras shoot twenty-four/seven. Even the stills add up quickly. And we store them for several months before deleting them."

"When we examined the stills after the two thefts," Gloria continued, "we saw a glowing, spherical white blur that appears out of nowhere and works its way up the gallery. The police call it an 'orb.' Then it works its way back, heading in the opposite direction, toward the museum entrance."

"Carrying the relics?" Pete asked.

"No," the dean replied. "Empty-handed." He stopped to consider his words, chuckling for the first time. "Weird, isn't it? Of course, orbs don't have hands, do they?"

3

A TECH TOUR

"Interesting," Pete said. "That suggests that the orb is not a disguise or costume, but some kind of technological illusion—like a projected image, maybe."

"Yes, somehow, someway," Dean Wasson replied. "It's worth noting that the ghost Roger spotted wandering around the floor appeared like it was really *there*. But ghost or no ghost—hands or no hands—our artifacts disappeared after the orb's second and third visits."

"How big is the orb?" Suzanne asked.

"Adult height, gliding over the floor."

Kathy sat up even taller in her chair. "Does it appear on the footage every time the ghost visits?"

"Well, there is a question as to whether the ghost our custodian saw—and the orb in the security stills—are one and the same," Gloria replied. "Roger thought the ghost was adult-size and human-shaped, but the orb is rather strange-looking and somewhat... rounder."

"But the answer to your question is 'yes,'" the dean interrupted. It was obvious the discussion had begun to vex him. His face had sagged, and he slumped lower in his chair. "The orb appeared on the night of each theft. But when Roger spotted the ghost, the security camera recorded nothing out of the ordinary. In fact, it recorded *nothing* while the ghost was on the premises. Eventually, we figured out the camera had somehow been disconnected—and then reconnected."

"Well, that's—that's darn near impossible," Tom stammered. "It would mean the thief has access to your security system."

"Yes, we considered that too," Dean Wasson replied. "And backing up that supposition, we changed the lock on the door to the control room after the first theft," Dean Wasson said. "Guess what? That failed at preventing the second theft."

"That points to an inside job," Suzanne said.

The dean shook his head in dismay. "Yes. That's exactly what the police said. Can you see our dilemma? The four of us have worked together for years. We know for a certainty—it's *not* one of us. The mystery is quite profound."

A few moments of wondering silence passed before Pete spoke up again. "Are the lights on at night?"

"Some are," Gloria replied. "Enough to see your way around without wasting energy. Normal in museums. I'd call it semi-dark. Kind of shadowy."

"Can we get access to the security stills?" Suzanne asked.

"Yes," Gloria replied. "I've copied all the relevant material onto a drive for you. It's ready to go."

"Any further questions?" Dean Wasson asked. The room fell silent once more. "Okay. I think we've spooked all of you enough. You've heard the entire sad story."

"Thank you, sir," said Tom. "That's a great overview. May we tour the museum?"

Everyone stood up, pushing their chairs aside. Kathy flipped her notebook closed.

"Follow me," Gloria said, motioning toward her office. "I'll grab a copy of the stills for you."

Dean Wasson shook hands with each of the young detectives. "I appreciate your help more than you can imagine. We must solve this crime. Otherwise, Yavapai Courthouse Museum will cease to exist."

"We'll do our best, sir."

"I have every confidence in you."

The foursome followed Gloria. After retrieving a flash drive from her office, she led them on a tour of the museum, beginning at the front entrance.

Inside the museum, just past the main double doors on the right, a locked narrow pocket door led to a tiny climate-controlled security room—so small that it looked more like a closet. Behind it, Gloria explained, was a dedicated computer and hardware that controlled the cameras, motion detectors, timers, and lighting.

She unlocked the door and slid it open. Everyone gathered around the tight space. Inside—taking up almost every square inch —was a black metal rack, six feet high, loaded with hardware from top to bottom.

Suzanne asked, "Who has the key to this door?"

"Just the four of us staffers, like the keys to the building and the security codes," Gloria replied.

"There's no camera focused here inside the front doors?" Tom asked.

"Not yet," Gloria replied. "As things turned out, that was an oversight on our part. We've ordered one, and I'm told it should arrive in Prescott within the next two weeks. Then we need to have it installed, of course. This is all a bit new for our small staff. In our old location on campus, our galleries were part of a much larger building, and the college itself provided our security."

Kathy wondered, "How do you turn the alarm system on and off?"

There was a small metal box on the wall, the size of a light switch. It sat at eye level, enclosed by an equally small metal enclosure. Gloria flipped it up to reveal an on/off switch.

"Right here," she replied. "Only takes a second, whether you're coming or going."

"So if you turn it off," Tom asked, "the motion detectors shut down. What about the cameras?"

"They keep running," Gloria replied, "including the two cameras on the front of the building."

The public displays were all arrayed on the museum's ground level in a full-floor gallery with a high, vaulted ceiling. The immense rectangular space divided into open display areas, some separated by chest-high partial walls. Colored checkerboard flooring further delineated the individual displays. The entire gallery—split down the middle by a central aisle—ran in a longish line down the length of the building, starting from the front entrance.

"The inside camera is right there," Gloria said, gesturing upward. Located high above the inside double glass doors, the camera aimed straight along the central aisle toward the back of the gallery. "Its wide-angle lens covers the entire space. Any thief gaining access through the main entrance would walk into the central aisle and be captured on stills in ten-second intervals. Also notice the rear emergency door." She pointed to the right side of the back wall. "The camera has a perfect angled view that includes that door."

Pete asked, "Are the camera stills stored here on your network?"

"Oh, no," Gloria replied. "Everything is in the Cloud."

As they ambled down the central aisle, Gloria pointed out a major security feature—all but invisible. "Hidden motion detectors surround each display."

Museum visitors traveled back in time from the front to the back of the gallery, beginning with recent history and progressing to the most ancient objects. Soon Gloria was leading her young guests past colorful exhibits portraying life-size models of early Arizona Native American families in everyday situations. Displays presenting ancient indigenous villages and homes, apparel, jewelry, pottery, weapons, methods of agriculture, and water sources and irrigation—a critical issue for desert dwellers—flowed elegantly from one display to another.

"Many of these relics are a thousand years old, and a few are up to *two* thousand years old," Gloria said with a hint of pride.

They strolled the gallery floor from front to back, winding around individual displays as the museum director explained their cultural significance. Pete noted that the historical importance and value of the relics increased as they worked their way toward the back of the gallery, where the oldest and most valuable Native American artifacts were proudly displayed, all lining the central aisle.

Just as they reached the second-last display, Gloria screamed. *"Oh, no, they're gone!"*

Within seconds the dean came pounding down the aisle. His pale face showed utter panic.

"The ghost has struck again!" Gloria cried out. *"Two of our Sinagua pots have vanished!"*

Dean William Wasson collapsed to the floor.

4

CRIME SCENE

Dean Wasson had crumpled just as he reached the pillaged display. Pete was closest to him—he attempted to break his fall, but the man tumbled to the floor with a heavy thud. On the way down, he nicked his head on the corner of a vitrine.

Gloria screamed again. She fell to both knees and grasped the dean's hand. "His skin is ice-cold!"

"He's unconscious," Kathy said tensely. Blood oozed out from a gash above his left eye.

"I tried to break his fall," Pete said. He gestured with his hands in dismay.

Tom checked the dean's pulse. His skin had turned clammy. "Suzie, call an ambulance."

Suzanne tapped 911.

"Call your dad too," Kathy said, gagging. She hated the sight of blood. Its stickiness always made her feel sick.

A distraught Gloria struggled for breath. The girls provided comfort, pulling a chair over. Tears ran down the director's face, smearing her mascara. Everything had happened so fast.

Minutes passed before Gloria recovered her composure. "I must call Jim Bright," she said, dabbing her eyes with a tissue. "He needs to get back here. This will be awkward."

Dean Wasson's assistant answered his cell phone in Phoenix. He was attending the second day of the regional convention for museum professionals but promised to return to Prescott right away.

Compared to Gloria, Jim Bright sounded surprisingly calm. "I should be there by early afternoon," he said over the speakerphone, his voice clipped. "Traffic won't be bad now."

Sirens wailed out front. A team of medics rushed in and soon roused the dean. They wheeled him out on a gurney, still groggy, and transported him to the emergency room at Prescott Regional Medical Center.

A few minutes passed as the reality of the situation set in. Suzanne wondered about the value of the missing artifacts. "How much are they worth?"

"No telling for sure," Gloria replied. "They're insured for four hundred thousand dollars but at auction they could fetch far more. That's common in our field. Few museums can afford to insure their most valuable objects for the highest prices they might command on the open market."

Tom whistled again. "So now we're approaching three quarters of a million dollars' worth of artifacts... *stolen*."

"At least," Gloria replied.

It wasn't long before a team of crime scene technicians descended upon the museum floor. They dusted the display for fingerprints.

"What good is that?" Kathy whispered. "Ghosts don't have fingers."

"This one doesn't even have hands," Suzanne replied with a grin.

A photographer captured stills and shot video too. The techs checked for broken glass or other signs of a break-in. One officer spoke over the phone with a representative of the security company.

There wasn't a physical clue anywhere.

Detective Joe Ryan, someone the twins had known since childhood, followed minutes later. He was a low-key investigator with a well-deserved reputation for solving crimes. "The best man on the force," the Chief said more than once.

A shortish individual of little hair and few words, the popular detective wore a rumpled suit and scuffed loafers. Thick glass lenses stood out from his face.

"Well, hello," he called out to the twins, his hand reaching out in greeting. "Good to see y'all again." He spoke with a pronounced southwestern drawl.

The twins introduced him to their best friends.

"We've heard about you forever," Pete said as he and Kathy shook hands with the veteran investigator.

Gloria led everyone to her office where they gathered around her computer screen. She downloaded the most recent digital image files from the Cloud, saving them to her desktop. She scanned to 02:04:10 a.m. from the night before, when a glowing white blur materialized on-screen—the orb, adult-sized, rounder, pulsating and floating over the floor.

"Freaking strange," Pete muttered, almost to himself.

"Look," Gloria said. "There it is, at the exact same time once again. At least the thing is consistent."

A few frames later, the orb was heading back down the central aisle, carrying nothing, toward the front doors. Gloria zoomed in on the still that followed the orb's vanishing act, showing the empty display cases where the two Sinagua pots had rested. "It doesn't seem to take anything, but they're gone all the same," she said, puzzled.

"What *is* it really, I wonder?" Suzanne asked.

"The ghost strikes again," Gloria said, her voice catching.

"There's no such thing," the detective commented dryly.

Tom scrunched up his face in silence. It was baffling.

Just then, Roger Holloway stuck his head into Gloria's office. His schedule normally called for cleaning early in the evening, right after the museum had shut down for the day. This morning he had rushed to work early.

"I heard about the burglary on the radio," he explained. "So I placed a 'closed' sign on the front doors on my way in."

"Oh, thanks, Roger," Gloria replied. "That never crossed my mind. Let me introduce you."

Mr. Holloway spotted the orb on Gloria's screen. "He sure looks different than the ghost I saw."

"We're aware of that," Gloria responded, her voice breaking again. The stress worked on her. "But that's what we see on the security footage."

Mr. Holloway was a short man in his sixties with wispy gray hair and a large belly. Thick suspenders served as resting places for his thumbs. He wore baggy pants and sneakers. Dark circles appeared under his eyes.

Detective Ryan had apparently interviewed the custodian regarding the earlier thefts. "We meet again," he said to Mr. Holloway, shaking hands. "Nothing unusual last night?"

"Not a thing."

"What time did you leave?"

"Midnight, same as I always do."

"The alarm was on, I assume?"

"Of course it was." Mr. Holloway bristled, his face turning a blotch red. "Do you think I'd forget to lock up and set the alarm?" His nostrils flared.

5

THE ANOMALY

The next two hours passed in a blur. Discussions centered upon the differences between a ghost and an orb, but what mystified everyone was how the thief gained access to the museum. They checked every door and window, looking for a clue—*anything*—that would suggest an entry point.

"And exit," Kathy. "He escaped too."

As twelve o-clock approached, Gloria ordered ham, turkey, and chicken sandwiches brought in for lunch.

Then, early in the afternoon, Jim Bright, pulled into a parking place and hurried into Gloria's office. He gave the director a big hug.

"I'm so sorry, Gloria," he said, "but William will be fine. I called the hospital. He had a mild heart attack. The nurse told me he's resting and doing well. He'll be back to work before we know it."

Gloria perked up. "Oh, thank goodness. Positive news at last."

Mr. Bright was a lean man in his forties dressed in stone-white khakis and a short-sleeved sports shirt. He had dark, longish hair pushed away from his forehead and piercing blue eyes.

His Southwest Museum Association meeting badge—an entry pass for the convention's events—still hung around his neck.

The assistant director smiled. "Sorry about my casual clothes. This is what we wear to conventions these days."

After introductions, the assembled group discussed the most recent loss.

"It's a major disaster," Mr. Bright declared. "These artifacts come from the Sinagua people and date to 800 AD. They represent a rare early style unique to their artisans. The Sinagua disappeared six and a half centuries later. The relics represent a premier example of their culture."

"Gloria figures they're worth four hundred thousand dollars," Suzanne said, glancing at Mr. Bright for confirmation.

"That's possible," he replied. Hesitation crept into his voice. "But at auction they might sell for twice as much, or more, in my estimation. I'll get a picture for you."

He walked out to the office corridor with Roger Holloway trailing behind him. A minute later, Tom heard the momentary eruption of an angry voice, but no one else seemed to notice. The assistant returned alone.

"Here they are," Mr. Bright said, holding out two 8x10 prints. He even treated the object photos with care, and it was easy to see why. The images displayed tall pottery vessels in perfect condition. Some talented ancient artist had encircled the pots with abstract graphic patterns in muted colors.

"Beautiful!" Suzanne exclaimed.

Pete asked, "How well known are they?"

"Oh, these are famous for sure, at least among museums and private collectors in the Native American field," the assistant director replied.

"Jim, please address the press," Gloria begged. "I understand there's a small army of reporters camped out front. It's amazing how fast word gets around."

"They monitor our police radios," Detective Ryan explained.

Mr. Bright took over the media interviews, juggling print and television reporters gathered on the steps. The news had exploded. Three thefts had netted artifacts approaching three-quarters of a million dollars at a minimum. Stranger yet, a ghost was wandering around Yavapai Courthouse Museum, coming and going at will. Was it possible for a poltergeist to escape into the courthouse itself? What a story!

"How I wish we could keep this crisis out of the news," Gloria said. "If we don't solve this case, our reputation will greatly suffer. It jeopardizes everything we've worked so hard for. What a... well, what a horrible thing!"

"Maybe 'the thing' likes all the attention," Suzanne replied. "He— or she—craves it."

"Oh, I get it," Pete said. "And *that* could motivate another attempted theft, so it's a blessing in disguise. We need the thief to show up again so that we can catch him."

"It's possible," Tom said. "Clearly, this whole decoy ghost business is not a *normal* way to steal anything. But I think three quarters of a million dollars is one heck of an incentive."

Gloria just nodded, obviously impressed with the team's analysis but still deeply disturbed by the threat to the museum's survival. She made two digital copies of the night's camera stills, one for Detective Ryan, the other for the mystery searchers. The director had rebounded from the morning's dramatic events.

Kathy asked, "Do you need a ride home, Gloria?"

"No thanks," she replied. "I'll hang in here with Jim until the press departs. Then I'm going to the hospital to see William."

Detective Ryan had one last question. "So, the last two remaining Sinagua relics... I assume they're now the most valuable artifacts in the museum?"

"Well," Gloria replied, looking uneasy, "I would say yes. To the best of our knowledge, we have some of the earliest known pottery artifacts from the Sinagua people—anywhere. The remaining two items also date to 800 AD."

"What are they worth?"

"I'd guess three hundred thousand for the matched pair—and again, at auction, heaven only knows."

"Okay," the investigator said, locking eyes with her. "Just so you know, you're running out of time."

Alarm crept into her voice. "What do you mean?"

"I think it's obvious those remaining two Sinagua relics are on the thief's shopping list—or soon will be."

An angry look crossed Gloria's face. She flushed red. "We get that, Detective Ryan. We really do. But your job is to *solve* this crime and *protect* the museum. Our role is to present the cultural history of Arizona to every visitor. Dean Wasson is not about to hide our artifacts from the public, ghost or no ghost."

Gloria stood up and strode out of her office, the heels of her shoes clicking on the hard floor, without saying another word.

From behind his thick lenses, Detective Ryan blinked. Then he spoke, almost as if talking to himself, "Roger didn't return."

"Yeah, I think he left a few minutes ago," Tom said.

"He seems a little difficult to get along with," Pete said.

The detective's eyes met Pete's before he replied. "Don't ever judge a book by its cover. I made that mistake once."

"Two more rare Indian relics had disappeared into thin air," Suzanne said. "There's a charade going on, a 'ghost' of some kind. Then things got worse."

"Total chaos," Tom said. "And it happened so fast."

"I couldn't believe it. My hair stood straight up," Suzanne added. "But the good news is that it turned out to be a *mild* heart attack."

At dinnertime that evening, the twins were describing the day's dramatic events for their parents. Having a father who served as the city's chief of police came in awfully handy. Their mother, Sherri, a social worker who worked out of her home office, had joined in the discussion too.

"Too much for the poor man," she said. "He couldn't take the pressure. My heart goes out to him."

"You know what's *really* interesting? There's no way for the 'ghost' to get inside the museum," Tom said, stabbing the air for emphasis. "That place is tight as a drum. Without keys and an access code, it's impossible."

"Unless there is a real ghost," Suzanne said, "and it can walk through walls."

"Oh my word," Sherri said, drawing back.

The Chief looked at his daughter with an amused look. "You don't seriously believe that, I hope."

"Not at all," she replied, tossing her head flippantly. "But since it can't be a ghost, then who—or *what*—is it?"

Tom's eyes popped open. He reached for his cell phone and checked the time. It was the middle of the night.

Something troubled him. *Something was missing.*

He slipped out of bed and padded down to the family room, carrying his laptop under one arm. The hard, ceramic tile was cold on his bare feet. There was utter silence except for the rhythmic ticking of a mantel clock.

He opened the museum's security image files and connected his computer wirelessly to the large-screen TV. The flat surface lit up, bathing the room in a blue-white glow. A series of digital images appeared from the night of the most recent theft. They were fairly sharp, considering the low-light conditions.

Over the next hour, Tom scoured each frame, shifting backward and forward, over and over, searching for a single clue. Then he reviewed the frames recorded on the nights of the two earlier thefts, looking for similarities. Yes, the orb appeared—and disappeared—at the same second for each theft. And it moved the same way too. Yet Tom sensed that there were anomalies—some mysterious pattern, *something*—flickering at the edge of his vision. But he couldn't quite put his finger on it.

Sometime later, not long before dawn, he powered down and crept upstairs to bed, where he fell into a deep, restful sleep.

6

A SUBTLE CHANGE

The lead headline in Saturday morning's *The Daily Pilot* shouted, "Ghost haunts Yavapai Courthouse Museum!" A subhead read, "$25,000 reward."

The story gripped Suzanne right to the last paragraph: "A worldwide search is on for six missing relics, valued at more than $700,000 in total. Aztec College, the sponsor of the famous museum and its important collection of Native Arizonan artifacts, has offered a substantial reward for the capture of the thief or thieves and the return of the stolen items. When asked if the ghost could escape from the museum into Yavapai County Courthouse, Assistant Director Jim Bright stated that there is no such thing as a ghost."

Suzanne walked over to the stairwell and yelled up to her brother. "Wake up, sleepyhead! The paper's here and there's *big* news."

Tom jumped out of bed and raced downstairs.

"Aztec College is offering a huge reward," Suzanne teased, her eyes dancing.

Tom scanned the front page. "No kidding! Twenty-five grand is a bundle. They don't believe in ghosts either."

"If we solve this mystery…" Suzanne said, her eyes dancing.

"Why not?" Tom replied, reading his sister's mind. "We can chase the reward. But we'll have to stay ahead of Detective Ryan."

"Good luck with that," the Chief growled softly from the breakfast table.

Suzanne rushed into the kitchen and hugged her father. "Morning, Dad. Police officers can't collect rewards, but *we* can try, right?"

The Chief sipped his second cup of coffee before answering. "Sure, but I guarantee you Detective Ryan is *way* out in front."

Sherri poured milk on her cereal. "That's a nice photo of Dean Wasson."

A few minutes later the Brunellis called, newspaper in hand. Kathy couldn't have been more excited. "Did you see it? Imagine a twenty-five-thousand-dollar reward. *Let's get it,*" she added in a conspiratorial whisper.

Laughter rang out but Pete jumped at the opportunity. "No, really. We should go for it."

What was the next move?

"Let's check out the security camera stills," Tom suggested. "I was looking at them last night. There *has* to be a clue there."

They agreed to meet that evening at the Brunellis'. It was time to review the evidence.

THE JACKSON AND BRUNELLI KIDS HAD GROWN UP TOGETHER, attending St. Francis Elementary School in Prescott, where they met and became best friends. Today, the four were all students at Prescott High, out for summer vacation. The two families were exceptionally close.

The Brunellis' father, Joe, was a well-known magazine publisher. His popular monthly specialized in history and enjoyed a worldwide readership—in print and online. Pete and Kathy helped assemble the magazine, even producing many of the graphics, a part-time job they both loved.

Their mother, Maria, an emergency room nurse at Prescott Regional Medical Center, was famous for her Italian cooking. Weekends meant big, delicious pasta dishes at the Brunellis'.

Just the thought made Tom hungry. *"Mmm-mmm,* the best," he always said, whenever the twins stayed for dinner.

Kathy would agree. She secretly checked her weight, often too. "That's why this family faces the never-ending battle of the bulge. It's a continuous fight to stay slim."

Laughter flowed nonstop at the Brunelli household. Kathy's vibrant sense of humor was a gift from her mother. The mother-and-daughter team played off each other, keeping everyone in stitches.

The twins arrived at seven o'clock, right on schedule. Maria provided an update on Dean Wasson.

"He's doing well. I checked on him after the shift change today. He was sitting up in bed reading, in good spirits."

The good news cheered them all.

The story at the county courthouse had gripped the entire city. Joe and Maria joined the group in the living room. Ghosts are exciting—even if you don't believe in them.

Pete said, "So you think the security footage holds a clue?"

"I'm hoping—not that I found anything. Let's start with the most recent incident."

Tom fired up his laptop and connected to a large-screen monitor. He opened the file containing the stills from Thursday night. "Okay, I'm fast-forwarding to 02:04:00—that's a bit after two in the morning. Remember, the 'ghost' always appears at the exact same time."

Moments later, a pale white orb emerged on-screen, frozen in time, in the entrance area below the camera.

"E-e-ew," Maria exclaimed, shocked. *"What is that?"*

"It's a 'ghost,' Mom," Kathy replied. "Nice, huh?"

Pete grimaced.

"Now I'll take us through the next few frames, one at a time," Tom said.

The orb passed along the central aisle, through the gallery from front to back. Frame by frame, it changed size and shape, glowing and animated, floating onward as if it had a purpose in mind.

"*E-e-ew*," Maria repeated, sinking lower in her chair. "That thing is strange."

The tenth frame displayed the orb at the back of the gallery, in the Sinagua display area. As the next frame appeared, the orb had begun its return trip.

"Two artifacts have disappeared," Joe muttered.

Tom smiled to himself at the expression on everyone's face. "For sure. Okay, I'll click through the next few frames." The orb retraced its path along the central aisle, expanding as it approached the camera, pulsating as it changed size and shape.

"Even *scarier*," Maria observed.

Tom looked around the room. "What are we missing?"

Pete replied, "Two pots disappeared, but the orb isn't carrying them."

"It *can't* carry anything," Maria said, shaking her head. "The thing doesn't have arms."

Suzanne asked, "If the ghost didn't take them, who did?"

"That's the million-dollar question," Joe said.

"Or twenty-five thousand dollars, in our case," Kathy quipped, her eyes growing larger.

"Is that the clue?" Suzanne asked.

"I wish I knew," Tom said.

Twenty frames after making its appearance, the orb vanished.

Kathy's face showed her impatience. "Nothing makes sense. If this is an illusion, why bother?" She glared at the screen as Tom clicked through a few of the stills that followed the orb's departure. "*Wait!*" she shouted. "Stop. Something *is* different. Go back. Check out the time code."

Tom backed up to 02:04:00 and hit Play. Just as the orb made its appearance, the color and luminosity of the time code changed— very subtly, almost imperceptible to the human eye. Then, at

02:06:10, right after the orb vanished into thin air, the numbers reverted to their original hue and intensity.

"The color of the time code changed!" Suzanne exclaimed.

"And now it's back to its normal color," Kathy said, still riveted to the screen.

Tom couldn't believe he had missed it. "I must have run through that sequence ten times, but I wasn't looking at the time code. Good for you, Kathy." He handed his laptop to Pete. "Back it up, partner, and start over. Let's ignore the ghost and focus on the time code."

Maria wrinkled her nose in confusion. "I still don't quite get it. What does the code color have to do with anything?"

"It's obvious that someone must have *altered* it," Joe said.

"Maybe it was the ghost," Kathy bugged.

"I would say not," Tom replied. "More like a smart, highly-skilled technology person who happens to be a thief. But I'm guessing he made one mistake. In the process of brightening the images to make the orb glow, he brightened the *entire* image, including the time code. The pulsating orb was so distracting that we didn't notice that the *whole* image is a little brighter. Look." He clicked through the sequence again. He was right.

"How could he pull it *off?*" Pete asked, amazed. "I mean—getting these images into the museum's Cloud storage?"

"There's only one way," Tom suggested. "He would have had to breach the museum's firewall and hack into its system. My guess is the thief inserted a little piece of malware, a short program that uploads this sequence of orb stills from a remote computer."

"During every theft," Joe said, nodding. "Or even right after?"

"That's possible," Tom said. "Or he pre-programmed the sequence even before he arrived."

"Oh, I get it," Suzanne said, sitting up straight. "He *replaces* the stills captured and stored in the Cloud with ones he has created in advance. Wow—turns out this guy is brilliant."

"He's having fun too," Maria said, "at the museum's expense."

"*He* could be a *she*," Kathy noted.

"But *why?* Why bother?" Joe asked.

"My guess is that he's trying to throw off the investigation," Tom said. "If he leads people down a ghost hole, they'll get lost in the chase. Look how much time we're wasting on this orb thing."

"And as a bonus, he's creeping out the museum staff," Suzanne added.

"Let's check the footage from the earlier incidents," Pete said, rubbing his hands together.

They scanned security-camera stills from the two earlier thefts. Once again, at the exact second the ghost appeared, the time code's red color changed its hue, becoming slightly brighter and more orange. When the orb disappeared, the code reverted to its initial hue. Nothing jarring. In fact, unless someone pointed it out, few would ever notice.

"Wait a sec," Kathy said. "Tom, can you run all three sets of stills side by side?"

"You bet," Tom said. "It'll take a bit to set them up."

Watching the sequences in tandem revealed something else: they were identical. The orb followed the same path, changing size, shape and glowing the same way. *Every time.*

"He prepped everything in advance!" Pete crowed. "It's the same stuff."

Tom groaned, chagrined that he had missed the trick. "Okay. So what do we think?"

"Someone overwrote the security footage in the Cloud with a prerecorded sequence of doctored pictures," Suzanne said. "Three times."

"You know what that means?" Kathy asked.

"Yes!" Suzanne said. "That explains the purpose of the first break-in. The thief shot the footage for these orb stills. He set a camera up high to match the view from the security camera. Then he doctored the images."

"And rolled them out for the real thefts," Joe said, grimacing.

"Who could get in there to do all this?" Maria asked.

"Well," Pete replied, "Dean Wasson said only *four* people have keys and the access code to the museum."

"Dean Wasson, Gloria Waldner, Roger Holloway, and Jim Bright," Tom said. "One of them is the most likely suspect."

"Or the ringleader," Pete said.

"That's hard to imagine, isn't it," Kathy said. It wasn't a question.

Tom held firm. "They're the only ones with a key and the passcode."

"Unless there really *is* a ghost," Maria declared with a giggle.

"Mom…" Kathy glanced sideways at her brother.

Maria giggled again. "You guys aren't any fun at all."

Tom stood up. "There's one way to find out."

7

THE PHANTOM OF THE OPERA

On Sunday morning, the Jackson and Brunelli families attended church services together. Afterward, they met in the basement for coffee and doughnuts—a Sunday ritual.

Reverend Robert Clement, a good friend for many years, stopped at their table to say hello. The two families knew that, in rare cases, their pastor had performed an exorcism—the expulsion of an evil spirit from a person or place.

"Like from the courthouse museum?" Suzanne whispered.

"Wouldn't that be something?" Kathy replied, her voice hushed.

Maria had similar thoughts. "What does the Church teach about ghosts?" she asked him.

The reverend smiled. "Ah, you're thinking of the ghost in the county courthouse. That fellow has received lots of press, hasn't he?" He pulled out a chair and sat down with them for a few minutes, setting his coffee cup on the table in front of them. "Well, there's a ton of literature about the unquiet dead." Then he laughed out loud. "But I don't remember ever hearing about a ghost who steals valuable artifacts. I'm not sure we have a teaching on spectral theft."

"Told you," Pete nudged his sister.

THAT NIGHT, THE JACKSON AND BRUNELLI FAMILIES MET AT downtown Prescott's historic Opera House and enjoyed *The Phantom of the Opera*. The summer offering from a local production company had received excellent reviews. Coincidentally, the famous musical takes place at the *Paris* Opera in 1870. The phantom is a disfigured genius who composes all the scores and stories. He lives in the cellar beneath the opera house.

Kathy loved it. She had always dreamed of becoming a Broadway star and had played a major part in every school play for years. This year she had taken acting classes in the theater's summer education program—and *that* had opened other doors for her.

"Like, for example, two free tickets to *The Phantom of the Opera!*" she had announced weeks earlier with glee. "The best musical ever!"

Afterward, the musical's performers gathered outside with the stage manager, a friendly guy named Robert Burns. The crowd enjoyed the opportunity to meet and shake hands with the lead players. Then, with Mr. Burns' permission, Kathy led her family and friends backstage, which was normally off limits to visitors. They wandered through the show's final set, meeting a dozen different people responsible for the flawless execution of the major musical— a very ambitious project for the company.

Kathy proudly introduced the musical director, Guy Davidson, and the head audio technician, Philip Woodson, to her friends and family. The music had moved her so much. She had grown close to two brothers, Tom and Andy Hardiman, the two senior stagehands, who wandered over to say hi. The company's executive director, Bob Carlson, stopped by too. He had attended high school with the Chief, and the two friends reminisced over old times.

It was a sparkling night to remember.

ON MONDAY AFTERNOON, AFTER A PLANNING MEETING CONCLUDED, A disagreement erupted.

"Okay," Tom said. "Pete and I will stay overnight in the museum."

"Tonight and every night until the thief shows up," Pete said.

"Or whatever—*whom*ever—the heck it is," Tom said.

The boys loved to team up and sometimes hogged too much of the action for themselves.

"Wait a minute," Suzanne interrupted, tossing her head with indignation. "You're considering going in by yourselves? Without us?"

"Sure, why not?" Pete said

"Good luck with that," Kathy retorted.

Tom said, "You never know; it could be dangerous."

That remark earned him a withering look of scorn from his sister. Her anger boiled over in a heartbeat. "Listen, hotshot, I can handle myself better than you."

"Me too," Kathy said, equally miffed.

Suzanne took a deep breath and calmed down as they drew lots and chose rotating pairs. Surveillance would vary night by night and the twins were up first.

Gloria, the group had decided, was the second least-plausible suspect, after Dean Wasson. Always a good judge of character, Suzanne had no concern about keeping her in the loop. "Nothing to worry about. She'd never tell a soul."

Kathy called the museum director to fill her in on their plans—which thrilled Gloria to no end. "Great! You can use my key and I'll provide the passcode. With luck, you'll find a few answers. No one has a clue what's going on in there."

The director agreed not to tell any of the other administration staffers—Roger Holloway, Jim Bright, or Dean Wasson, who was still in the hospital. "We never talk business with him, on doctor's orders. I'll keep our secret from everyone else."

"That's fine—unless she has anything to do with it," Tom said, just as Kathy disconnected. "The thief won't be expecting us."

On Monday night, a few minutes before midnight, the twins parked down the street from the museum. They sat in silence, waiting patiently. It had only been three days since their meeting at Yavapai Courthouse Museum. *What could be next?*

The twins watched as Roger Holloway sauntered out, locked the front doors, and located his vehicle. Seconds later he drove away.

"Let's go," Tom urged, excited for the new adventure. Suzanne was already out of the car.

They hurried up to the front doors with their gear—sleeping bags, cell phones, flashlights, snacks, water, books, and magazines. Suzanne used Gloria's key and the five-digit passcode to enter the building. Then she locked the doors behind them.

Once they were in, Tom shut down the security system. "Suzie, you take the back of the gallery, I'll stay in front by the double doors. If one of us sees anything, we'll shout."

"Okay, got it." Either way was fine with her.

The twins separated and set up in their respective areas. They each dropped a sleeping bag on the floor inside an exhibit, hiding behind a partial display wall, making themselves comfortable for what promised to be a long night.

In the dead silence, they talked by raising their voices. Still, it was a lonely vigil. No thief appeared, but there were plenty of ghostly sounds. When it first starts up, *whooo, whooo* is a spooky sound.

"That's an owl!" Tom raised his voice.

"It sure is," Suzanne replied. "He's just outside the windows."

The bird of prey kept the twins' company for an hour. Legions of restless birds, cooing and rustling all night long, nestled in the trees surrounding the county courthouse.

Strangest-sounding of all was the wind, rattling around the dark old building. It gusted often, shaking windows and screens, scraping tree branches against the stone facade and creating an odd, screeching sound. Once they heard a door slam, which caused both twins to jump a foot off the floor.

"What the heck was *that?*" Suzanne cried out.

"My guess is, the wind," Tom replied.

They watched as 2:04 in the morning came and went. Fifteen minutes later, a powerful beam of light swept across the gallery floor. Tom crept over to a window to glimpse a police officer heading back to her vehicle. "Just a patrol officer doing a routine check," Tom said in a forced whisper. "She couldn't see us."

Suzanne laughed. "Good thing we didn't pop up. She might have arrested us!"

The night dragged on interminably. Often the twins encouraged one another to stay alert.

"Are you awake over there?" Suzanne called.

"Sure am. Do you think I'd sleep on the job?"

"Yuck, yuck."

It felt like an eternity. Finally, Suzanne had had enough. "Okay, let's get out of here. The thief is a no-show."

Tom glanced at his cell phone, yawning for the umpteenth time. It was 4:00 a.m., almost two hours after the thief's normal arrival. "Right on. I am *so* tired."

8

AN INTRUDER MATERIALIZES

On Tuesday night, it was the Brunellis' turn. Neither one was too excited.

"Oh, joy," Kathy complained to Suzanne on an earlier call. "A boring night calls—the big guy doesn't talk much, you know."

"I wonder why," Pete retorted in the background.

Still, something had to happen. It just *had* to.

They knew the drill. Pete parked down the block and watched until Roger drove into the night. Then they let themselves in and locked the doors. Kathy flipped off the alarm.

"You move to the back of the floor, I'll sack out here in front," Pete suggested.

"Whatever."

Pete threw his sleeping bag onto the floor of an exhibit beside the central aisle, just feet from the control system, then arranged the rest of his gear.

Minutes later Kathy called out, "Everything good?"

"You bet," Pete replied. "But if you see anything strange, hoot like an owl."

His sister giggled. "How about if I scream?"

"If you give yourself away, we're in big trouble."

Time dragged in slow motion. Pete's eyes grew heavy. He pinched himself more than once, trying everything he could to stay awake before 2:04 came... and went. *No show,* he thought. He drifted off into a dream. A weird grinding sound played, followed by silence. Somewhere a flashlight clicked on.

Pete awoke with a start and sat straight up, his pulse racing. A beam of light bounced before vanishing an instant later.

What's happening? And why now?

A strange voice, a man's, low and close, muttered one word, "What...?"

No way to signal Kathy or call out to her. In fact, he could hardly *breathe* without alerting the thief.

A rustling noise caught his attention. Something draped in white glided along the central aisle, passing Pete where he lay tensed on the floor. *The ghost. The one that Roger had first spotted.*

As it passed by, dark shoes bobbed out beneath the whiteness. Pete leapt up and bolted out of the exhibit. He tackled the ghost, going straight for its legs. Then everything went black.

LATER, MUCH LATER IT SEEMED, KATHY'S VOICE CALLED OUT FROM A long, dark tunnel, a million miles away. She shook him. *"Wake up, Pete.* Wake up!"

Pete's eyes flickered as he lay on the floor, face up. His sister's face appeared, upside down and staring at him from a crazy angle. Bright fluorescent lights burned overhead. Something throbbed with pain. He reached up to discover a huge, sensitive bump on the crown of his head. *What am I doing here?*

"Are you okay?" Kathy asked, freaked.

"Not really." Confused and disoriented, his mind refused to focus. "What happened?"

"Good question! Noises woke me up—a squeal and then a strange grinding sound. It took me a bit to remember where I was. I looked down the aisle and there you were—laying flat on your back and not moving a muscle. Did you jump the guy?"

Pete shook his head. Gently. "Oh, yeah... yeah, that's right. I tackled him. He must have hit me with something. Did I conk out?"

"Did you ever. I raced over after the commotion, but he was long gone. Why didn't you yell out?"

"I-I dunno," he stammered, his mind refusing to focus. "Too dangerous, I guess."

Someone rattled the front doors.

"Is that the thief?" Pete stood up, grabbing his sister's arm for support. He was unsteady, and his headache throbbed even worse.

"I doubt it," Kathy said. "More likely the police. I turned the gallery lights on."

Sure enough, a local patrol officer was trying to gain access. Kathy unlocked the front doors to greet a wary Officer Kate Branson. It wasn't often the policewoman heard a tale like this one, but the "ghost" in the county courthouse had become famous—the whole city knew.

"Okay, I believe you," she said, after hearing the Brunellis' account of the night's events. "This is a crime scene now—*again*. I'll get things rolling."

Twenty minutes later, the Chief and Joe Brunelli were standing beside Pete and Kathy in the museum. "You sure you're okay, Pete?" his father asked.

"Well, he gave me a big thump on my head, but I'm fine. Does anyone have an aspirin?"

Detective Ryan arrived next, dressed in his trademark rumpled suit. "Congrats," he said, shaking hands with the brother and sister. "Welcome to my world."

The twins appeared, perturbed to have missed the grand adventure. Suzanne had heard her father leave the house. She woke Tom up and the two rushed to the museum.

"Nice work if you can get it," Suzanne grumbled to her friends.

Tom laughed, playfully slugging Pete. "You have all the fun."

"Oh... Sure. Like this little souvenir, for example," Pete said, bending over to show the lump on his head. It still throbbed painfully.

"Ouch," Suzanne said, grimacing. "That *is* ugly."

The three men seemed excited.

"It's the idea of a ghost," Kathy confided. "Almost everyone reacts the same way."

The group began an extensive search of the gallery. A minute passed before Kathy found a man's shoe—size twelve—beneath a table vitrine, just inside the display area. Right where Pete had been sleeping before he sprang out and tackled the intruder.

A smile crossed the Chief's face. "Well, look at that. The ghost wears shoes. Men's, size twelve. He's a big fellow."

"It must have fallen off when you tackled him, Pete," Suzanne said. "Excellent job."

"A major clue," the detective muttered. "About time."

"One thing," Pete mentioned. "Before he started down the aisle, the ghost said something."

"A ghost that talks too," the Chief said, chuckling. "What did he say?"

"He said, 'What?'"

"That's it? One word?"

"Yup. It was like an unfinished sentence—an unfinished *question*."

"Interesting," said the detective. "Something surprised him. I wonder what it was?"

"Bet I know," Tom said, looking at the Brunellis. "You had deactivated the alarm. He couldn't figure out why it was off. Must have been quite a shock."

Detective Ryan grunted, seemingly impressed but trying not to show it.

"Something else, too," Pete said as he rubbed the crown of his head. "The ghost missed his 2:04 time slot. He came a few minutes later."

"That's a first," the detective said, puzzled.

"Where did our ghost with one shoe go?" Joe wondered.

A search in the museum, including its large entrance area, turned up no other clue.

The detective shook his head. "Well, there's no sign of his presence. No forced entry, no broken glass, nothing disturbed. Plus a locked front door and a secured emergency back door. Once again, the thief disappeared into thin air—"

Kathy stopped him. "Let's check the security footage," she said.

9

A CLOSER LOOK

"I'll call Gloria," Suzanne said.

"Tell her we'll send a patrol car to pick her up," the Chief said.

Fifteen minutes later the museum director arrived, casually dressed in jeans and a jacket. Everyone trooped into her office and gathered around her screen. Gloria downloaded the stills from the Cloud, starting at 02:04:00. Attentive and wide-eyed, they sat back, riveted to the screen as the orb floated up and down the gallery's central aisle.

"There you go," Pete said, his voice dripping with scorn. "Someone doctored the entire sequence. What's interesting is that he arrived later than the time code shows. And he didn't appear that way at all—he's basically a big guy in a bedsheet. Plus, the camera doesn't show me tackling the intruder."

"Or me rushing over to help," Kathy added.

"So," Suzanne added, "what we're seeing here was edited in advance, top to bottom."

Tom nodded yes. "Nothing is real."

"But when the orb disappears, the security camera kicks back in and records normally," Detective Ryan said, almost as if talking to himself. On the screen, Kathy reached down to Pete and helped him to his feet. "This is one high-tech-savvy thief. How does he do it?"

"That brings up something interesting," Suzanne said, glancing at the two officers. "Gloria, please click through the stills once more. Keep your eyes on the time code, everyone."

As in the older reviewed frames, the numbers changed color and intensity during the thief's incursion. Gloria ran through the sequence twice before Detective Ryan caught the change.

"The time code changes color," he said in a flat, unemotional voice.

"*Exactly,*" Kathy replied with a smile.

"You picked up on that?" the Chief asked. "Impressive."

Tom nodded. "Kathy spotted it first. That's what tipped us off. There *had* to be a tech-savvy someone doctoring the stills ahead of time."

"Same thing in the previous thefts?" Gloria asked.

"Yes! See for yourself," Suzanne said.

Gloria opened the older files. Frame by frame, they all watched as the strange orb floated along the gallery floor. Each time, the code change was subtle—but unmistakable.

Gloria returned to the most recent attempt, an hour earlier. She froze the screen on the image of the Sinagua display cases after the orb had vanished and zoomed in tight. Seconds later the two beautiful vases reappeared, safe and sound.

"So there it is," Gloria said. Her eyes darted to the Brunelli siblings. "He would have taken those artifacts too—if it hadn't been for you."

Kathy grinned. "Give the twins credit," she said graciously. "We've all been taking turns camping out here."

"I'll tell you something, that thief was a lot more solid than an orb of light," Pete said. His head still ached.

"Now we have a solid theory to help us identify the thief," Detective Ryan said.

"Yes," Tom said. "Whoever this person is, he altered the security footage by creating a sequence of doctored stills. Then he hacks into the museum's system and embeds the faked material—it replaces the stills recorded during each theft by the inside camera—*before* he even breaks in."

"Bottom line," Kathy said, "he created this 'orb' thing to throw everyone off-track."

"And to intimidate our entire museum staff," Gloria exclaimed, "Oh my gosh, that explains a lot!"

"Sure," Suzanne said, nodding. "Including why the time code changes at the exact same moment. To make his job easier, he's reusing the same sequence of doctored stills based on footage shot in advance. That explains the first break-in when he stole nothing... when he shot his raw 'ghost' footage."

"If you compare the sequences in parallel," Pete added, "you can see that the orb stills are always identical—except for the last one, showing the empty display cases. The creepy images distracted us, which is why we didn't notice at first. The only change is which artifacts he intends to steal."

The Chief added things up. "He keeps coming back, which suggests that the thief, or the ringleader of his gang—has found a buyer, or a fence—someone to sell the artifacts on the black market. He makes the sale first, then returns to steal the artifacts. But tonight he failed for the first time, thanks to our young mystery searchers here."

"Who is he?" Gloria asked. "How does he get in here? And where does he go?"

The detective chuckled. "Well, Gloria, those are tough questions. First things first. We know it isn't you."

Laughter burst out around the room. Kathy rushed over and gave the museum director a hug. "Well, thank goodness for that," Gloria replied.

"And Dean Wasson isn't a suspect," the Chief added. "He's still in the hospital."

"That leaves Roger Holloway and Jim Bright hanging out there," Gloria said. Her voice caught a little. "They're the only others with keys and the passcode."

"That's true," the detective said. "But I've run extensive background checks on both men. Neither of them has the requisite skills to pull off these thefts. And without doubt, Roger Holloway doesn't have the connections needed to sell stolen artifacts."

"Jim Bright might have those, as a longtime museum professional," Kathy said.

"True," Detective Ryan said, "but he wasn't in town during the last two burglaries. Both men's alibis check out, dates and time."

"Plus, both gentlemen are too small to wear a size-twelve shoe," Tom noted.

"Neither one is the thief," Suzanne concluded, "but that doesn't mean they're not involved."

"I still need more time to investigate," Detective Ryan said.

"Don't forget," Pete said. "The thief doesn't need a key and passcode for the front door. *Or* a key for the security closet."

"Well, how does he get in?" Kathy asked.

The detective blinked several times. "Ah, good question. There's no sign of forced entry. The windows and doors are all intact. And he can't walk through walls." He grinned. "It's a real conundrum."

10

A SECRET FROM THE PAST

That Wednesday morning, the four mystery searchers grabbed a few hours of sleep before descending upon the offices of *The Daily Pilot*. Heidi Hoover had agreed to a meeting after an early call from Suzanne. The star reporter had been editor at Prescott High's newspaper in her senior year—the same year the four started junior high. They didn't really know Heidi, but she had covered the story of the mystery on Apache Canyon Drive. Quite well, in fact.

It hadn't taken long before she became a huge fan. "You guys don't give up easily. I like that."

They met in a large conference room at the newspaper's head-quarters. "Okay, what's up?" she asked, after greeting the foursome. Known for her rapid-fire way of speaking, Heidi rarely minced words.

"Well," Suzanne began, "we're working on the mystery of the ghost in the county courthouse."

That sent Heidi into her trademark giggle. Tight black curls bounced around her head. "That's awfully funny, you realize that, right?"

"I know," Suzanne said, laughing with her. "We don't believe in spooks either."

"But here's the thing," Tom explained. "Somehow the thief is getting into the museum despite high-security doors and windows."

"So," Pete said, "maybe he's walking through walls."

"Or doors or floors," Kathy added, looking quite earnest.

"What we're wondering," Suzanne asked, "is there anything about local history in the newspaper's archives that could give us a clue?"

"Like the courthouse's construction," Tom thought aloud. "Is there something that time has forgotten? Or a thief who broke in in the past, before it became a museum. Or *anything*? We're at a loss."

Heidi jumped to her feet. "Okay, got it. Follow me, let's go see what we can find."

The newspaper had been in operation since 1881. Much of its newer material was stored in digital form, but the earlier years' editions were accessible only on microfilm: the bound volumes of the older copies were all printed on high-acid newsprint. They were too fragile to examine.

Heidi led her guests into a central archival room. "We tag each story with keywords," she explained. "Use this computer to search for them. If there's a match, it'll pull up specific headlines with matching dates."

"For example," she typed as the foursome gathered around her, "let's try *courthouse* plus *construction*." Forty-three headlines appeared, with a date, section, and page reference beside each one. "If it's pre-2000, you'll find that day's entire edition on a single microfilm, stored on those shelves." She pointed to rows of metal bins. "In which case, you load the film and scan to the page number you're looking for. See? Simple, right?"

Heidi's cell phone rang. She glanced at the incoming caller. "Uh-oh, gotta run, have fun," and she was out the door. "Call me if you find something interesting!" she called back from halfway down the hall.

The foursome looked at one another. "We could be here for hours," Suzanne groaned.

"Well, let's reason this out first," Tom suggested. "The thief is *not* breaking through the windows."

"Nor through the front double doors, or the emergency door at the back," Pete said.

"He isn't walking through walls, either," Kathy half joked.

"We don't think he has a copy of the keys and codes—at least, the museum staff say that's impossible," Suzanne said.

"What about coming through the ceiling or floor?" Tom asked. "What was on site before the courthouse came out of the ground?"

A quick search of the archives showed that the courthouse was the second structure erected on the site. The first courthouse had burnt to the ground.

Tom shook his head, filtering the information. "Okay, so what. That was more than a century ago. Is there something odd about the old sewer pipes under the building? No wait, not the sewer, a tunnel! Search for *tunnels.*"

Tom keyed in *tunnels* and related key words: *passages, excavations, digging.* Twenty minutes slipped by before Suzanne suggested another variation of the theme. "Try *secret tunnels,*" she said. Fifteen hits popped up—all pre-2000. "Now we're cooking."

The boys turned toward the microfilm shelves, but Kathy interrupted.

"Wait a sec. Narrow it down further. Type in *secret tunnels downtown,*" she prompted. Pete tapped the keyboard. Only five dates popped up. Three of them were from 1927, one was from 1936, and the most recent dated to 1947. Four of the five articles appeared to center on William Clark, who had reigned like a king as Prescott's mayor from 1920 until 1932. He had died in 1936.

"Let's start with 'forty-seven and work backward," Kathy suggested.

Pete loaded the microfilm into a reader. They found a headline reading "Prescott's chief engineer discovers secret tunnel." A grainy old black-and-white picture displayed a large man with a handlebar mustache standing in a seven-foot-high tunnel, his arms extended from wall to wall. The article read, "Nate Parsons, the city's chief engineer, announced the discovery of an underground tunnel during the repair of a water main on Whiskey Row. It was a hundred feet long and appeared to have been dug earlier in the century. The tunnel had caved in at both ends decades before. City workers resealed the breakthrough. No further information is available."

"Can you believe it?" Pete exclaimed. "So there *was* at least one tunnel downtown, for sure." His voice dropped into a conspiratorial tone. "We're on to something."

Suzanne loaded the next microfilm. The 1936 headline read, "Mayor William Clark dies." The obituary detailed the mayor's successful life from birth to death, emphasizing his dedication to the city. But what captured their attention was the final paragraph. Suzanne read it aloud. "'For years, Mayor Clark denied the existence of a network of secret underground tunnels in Prescott's downtown area. In the nineteen-twenties, his administration was accused of turning a blind eye to the possible existence of the tunnels, reportedly built to transport liquor to Whiskey Row. Suspicion remained, because such an operation would have been enormously profitable in the Prohibition era. However, no tunnels ever came to light.'"

"Well, that's intriguing," Kathy said. "They were running liquor!" The foursome high-fived one another.

"Yes, they were," Tom said. *This was it.* "Not a shred of doubt. There is—or was—one tunnel. Maybe more than one."

Whiskey Row and its infamous history were well documented. After a fire burned down an entire downtown block in 1900, the neighborhood quickly resurrected. Some forty saloons sprang up, and the street soon earned its moniker of Whiskey Row. Fifteen years later, Prohibition began early in Arizona. But the liquor business in Prescott continued to boom. Bars were forced to close or change into other kinds of businesses, but "ice cream parlors"—the local nickname for speakeasies—had continued to operate, serving liquor in a back room or downstairs, in the basement. Local authorities looked the other way.

The two earlier stories exposed the rumors of illegal tunnels and their connection to Whiskey Row liquor smuggling. Mayor Clark and his administration denied both.

"He fibbed," Kathy said. "Bet he was in on the scam, getting a piece of the profits."

"In exchange for instructing the police to look the other way," Pete said.

"Who cares!" Suzanne exclaimed. Excitement ringed her voice. "We need to talk to whoever the city engineer is today."

11

A SHOCKING REVELATION

Bill Holden, the city's chief engineer, was easy to find... no problem—but pinning him down was tougher.

"Too busy," he replied to Suzanne when she introduced herself over the telephone. "Call me back in two weeks."

"We can't wait that long, Mr. Holden," she insisted. "We think we've discovered the existence of an underground tunnel, and it's very important that we meet now."

A sudden pause in the conversation ticked past before his voice came back, sharp and distinct. "*What* did you say?"

"An underground tunnel," Suzanne repeated. "We know there's one downtown, and we need help finding it."

The man's tone changed in a heartbeat. "When did you wish to meet?"

"How about right now?" she shot back..

"Whoa," Kathy whispered, listening in the background. "Something's going on."

At five o'clock that same afternoon, the foursome traipsed into Bill Holden's City Hall office. A tall, square-jawed man, he displayed a friendly, easy demeanor. He had cleared his desk before they arrived. And he had done his homework.

"Well, a pleasure to meet you," he said, shaking hands with each of them. "Call me Bill. I followed your exploits on Apache Canyon Drive. That must have been quite the adventure. How can I help?"

Suzanne opened the discussion, asking Bill to keep the subject confidential.

"Oh, sure, I understand," he replied, but at the mention of tunnels his eyes blazed. "Mayor Clark denied those rumors during Prohibition. He was *flat-out wrong*."

The mystery searchers glanced at one another.

"Wrong? What do you mean?" Tom quizzed.

"Well, it turns out there *was* a tunnel," he replied, "and we stumbled into it a few weeks ago—on April fifteenth, to be exact. While replacing old water pipes on Whiskey Row, the city team punched through an earthen ceiling by accident. The team darn near fell into an underground passage. *Amazing.* The excavation was in front of the first building off Montezuma and Gurley Streets. Hang on, let me show you."

Bill strode out of his office and soon returned with a massive rolled-up document. "Here, give me a hand."

The four jumped up to help unroll a downtown survey map, which opened to a width of six feet. They attached the map to a large foam board that covered one wall, then gathered around the animated chief engineer.

"Okay, the business is here," Bill said, jabbing at a corner structure on the chart. He drew a large red X on the building. "It's called the Wild West Bar."

"Oh, sure, I've seen the place," Tom said. "You'd never forget that name. We must have passed by it a thousand times."

A hint of a smile crossed Bill's face. "Then you passed right over the tunnel. Every time too. You didn't realize it, and neither did anyone else. A bar has occupied that building for well over a hundred years—sometimes legal, other times not. The tunnel came from the east and opened into the bar's basement."

The chief engineer drew a line on the map, starting at the red X and crossing Yavapai Street. After a slight rightward jog, the line extended deep into the grassy four-acre park—pointing toward the county courthouse.

Bill used his large hands to show the tunnel's size. "It's seven feet high and wide enough for two or three grown men to pass through. A real feat of engineering for the time—even more if they dug it in secret. What did they do with all the earth they excavated? We'll never know."

"Where did the tunnel end up?" Pete asked, holding his breath.

"We couldn't tell for sure," Bill replied, eyeing his visitors and enjoying every second of the meeting. His face radiated excitement. "We hit an impassable cave-in, about right here." He drew a big red X on the park, well short of the museum. "So that's a mystery. But notice it aims toward the county courthouse. It's a good bet the tunnel extended that far originally. We assume smugglers used it to funnel illegal liquor to the bars on Whiskey Row. That was the rumor back then. No telling, a century later."

"Corruption must have been rampant," Kathy said.

"Yes, indeed," Bill agreed. "That happened a lot under Prohibition—there was so much money sloshing around." His audience was all ears. "But get this. There was another mystery the day we discovered the tunnel—a strange, unbelievable one. We found footprints down there—*fresh* ones too. We weren't the first ones in."

"Well, that's downright spooky," Suzanne said. Goosebumps traveled up and down her back. "Who would *they* belong to?"

"Your guess is as good as mine," he answered.

Silence fell before Kathy had a question. "You mentioned that the tunnel opened into the basement of the bar. Was the opening hidden behind a wall?"

"Nope," the engineer replied. "We reached a set of stairs going up. An old black-painted metal lever activated an entrance in the basement floor. When we yanked the lever, a hidden trapdoor disguised as a paver opened upward," he chuckled. "It squealed like crazy before knocking over a case of whiskey. That brought the Wild West owner rushing down. Charlie Watts is his name. He figured we were there to steal his liquor."

The chief engineer grinned, accentuating his square jaw. "We shocked the heck out of him, no doubt. From his basement, the tunnel was impossible to detect. Talk about weird. At first we didn't have a clue where we were."

"If you were trying to enter the tunnel from the basement," Tom asked, "what triggered the trapdoor to open?"

The man bent closer, relishing every disclosure. "It was ingenious. We tried everything before we figured it out. When you press down on two diagonally opposite corners of the paver simultaneously, the thing pops open—bottom left, top right. That's the only way it works. Big enough for a large man to duck under. The old wooden stairs were in rough shape, but still intact."

Bill's eyes continued to dance as he told the story. "Just think. The entrance lay hidden for darn near a century. The current owner of the bar has used the basement for storage over the past twenty-five years." His voice dropped. "It never once crossed his mind that a secret passageway was right under his feet."

"Is it possible that other tunnels exist?" Suzanne asked.

"Sure, why not?" Bill mused. "There's one, for sure. It's easy to imagine that there are more down there, paralleling the water and sewer tunnels—beside them but invisible. It was a freak accident that we broke through the earthen ceiling like that."

"Can we get into the tunnel?" Kathy asked.

"Nope, too dangerous," the chief engineer replied, straightening up and shaking his head. "We only went down once. The timbers holding it up have rotted out in many places. More cave-ins are inevitable."

"What about getting into the basement?" Pete asked. "Could we see how the secret entrance works?"

"Oh, sure," Bill said, "I can arrange that. I'll call the Wild West's owner. But whatever you do, stay away from that tunnel."

"Why did you keep the discovery a secret?" Suzanne wondered aloud.

"Orders to hold off from the boss," Bill replied, pointing upstairs. "Mariana—Mayor Hernandez, that is. Until she puts her stamp of approval on a press release, coming soon. 'I'd rather the past be the past,' she said, 'but the public has a right to know.' It's kind of funny, since Mayor Clark denied any possibility of secret tunnels. He was the one person responsible for putting an end to the rumors. Back then, the newspapers were full of it."

"We read all about it in the archives at *The Daily Pilot*," Tom said.

"Yup, it was a big deal," Bill continued. "Now we know there *was* a tunnel—maybe more. We believe Mayor Clark *had* to know the tunnels existed, and so did other members of his administration. That means he, uh, fibbed."

The chief engineer paused. He leaned forward again. A strange look crossed his face. "The final nail in the coffin is this: during Prohibition, Mayor William Clark's office was on the ground floor of Yavapai County Courthouse… right where the museum is today."

12

THE PHANTOM

The owner of the Wild West Bar offered a tour the next morning, Thursday, long before opening.

"Hello, everyone!" Charlie Watts swung the front door open from inside, and the foursome trooped into the dark, chilly bar. "I didn't realize that we'd have such a large party. Welcome, welcome." He offered his hand. "My friends call me Charlie." A short, stocky, middle-aged man with little hair and huge arms, he looked the part of a bar owner. He wore a white apron tied around his ample waist. Introductions followed.

Charlie was a gregarious man with a hearty laugh and a talkative, open manner. "Very pleased to meet you! So, our big secret is out, huh? Well, it was only a matter of time."

Just then Detective Ryan walked in. He carried a large lantern flashlight in one hand and a camera in the other. "And this is Detective Ryan," Suzanne said. "Detective Ryan, Charlie Watts." The two men shook hands.

Charlie unlocked the door to a stairwell and flipped on the light, a single bare hanging bulb at the foot of a wide staircase descending into a drab, gloomy basement. He led the way. "Come on down, folks."

Everyone trooped downstairs as a musty smell filled their nostrils. The bartender paraded his guests past dozens of boxes stacked five and six feet high. A dozen more—empty—cluttered the basement floor, scattered at random.

Old stone pavers covered the floor, each measuring three feet square, like giant tiles.

"That's the one," Charlie said, pointing toward a paver in the middle of the floor. A heavy stack of full boxes rested on it. With little effort he slid the stock to the side.

"They all appear identical," Tom commented, kneeling to examine the stone flooring.

"Yes, they do," the owner replied. "That's why we never noticed."

The others scanned the pavers, each of which was bordered by thin metal strips on all sides. A few chips stood out, but nothing that drew attention.

"Can you show us how it opens?" Kathy asked.

"Sure. Stand back."

Charlie knelt, stretched out his arms, and pushed down hard on two diagonally opposite corners of the paver. With a slight grinding sound, squealing as it rose, the trapdoor lifted away from the floor.

Pete recognized the sound: the same weird noise that had awoken him in the museum.

Charlie stood and backed away from the opening. Four rusty metal bars, one at each corner, raised the hidden trapdoor four feet into the air before it shuddered to a stop.

Seconds passed in total silence. The group gaped into a yawning shaft. Pete, an aspiring engineer, reached out and touched one of the rusty metal bars. "That's quite an engineering feat."

"Yup," Charlie said, chuckling. "Unbelievable, right? It works on a mechanism triggered by equal weight bearing down on both those corners. The city guys said it was a good bet the trapdoor hadn't moved since Prohibition ended in 1933. Imagine that."

The foursome sprawled out and peered down into the shaft. Detective Ryan knelt and clicked on his lantern, shooting a powerful beam onto the tunnel floor. Old wooden stairs led to the bottom, a dozen steps down.

"Just as Bill Holden described," Suzanne said.

"Looks lonely down there," Kathy said.

Pete peeked down, remembering an awful night on Apache Canyon Drive when he had found himself trapped in a stifling, smelly industrial dumpster full of shredded printed paper. Claustrophobia had set upon him for the first time. Not good. Now, as he peered down into the narrow shaft, the feeling returned. His breathing quickened. His chest grew tight.

"Nothing there but dirt," Charlie said.

"Did you go into the tunnel?" Tom asked.

"Oh, sure," the bar owner replied, "same day the excavation team appeared. We walked it together, from here to the cave-in. It was an amazing experience."

Detective Ryan quizzed him. "Did you notice anything interesting?"

"Well, I spotted footprints going both ways, to and from the cave-in," Charlie replied. "You couldn't miss them, because there was an inch-thick layer of dust along the way."

The four murmured in agreement. "Sure, that makes sense," Suzanne said. "The excavation team left footprints everywhere."

"They did," Charlie said, "but the city folks trekked *west*, from the excavation point straight to my basement. That's when they scared the heck out of me. A few minutes later I toured the tunnel with them, and we headed *east*."

He paused and surveyed the faces around him. His audience hung on to every word.

"We reached the excavation point. I looked up and saw daylight. The water-pipe-laying team members had flashlights. Beams of light flashed everywhere, including on the tunnel floor. Bill Holden said, 'Let's keep going.' Well, that's when I spotted one set of footprints heading in each direction. I asked him, 'Didn't you guys go up there?' 'Not yet,' he replied. 'Let's do it.' So we did. We followed the prints from the excavation point to the cave-in."

"Bill mentioned those strange footprints," Suzanne said.

Charlie stopped again, shaking his head at the thought. "There's no doubt someone else had toured that tunnel before the excavation team showed up. One set of footprints headed west, coming my way. A second set traveled east. We don't know who they belonged to, but we darn sure know when they appeared."

Detective Ryan, a low-key man of few words, seldom displayed surprise. Today was no different. "What makes you say that, Charlie?" he asked neutrally.

In response the owner turned, cupped his hands around his mouth and yelled, "Dick, are you upstairs?"

A tall, thin man appeared at the top of the stairwell.

"Come on down," Charlie urged. "These people are interested in the phantom. Folks, say hello to Dick Hearne, the world's finest bartender."

Dick joined them on the basement floor. The bartender looked close to fifty years of age, bald and clean-shaven, wearing a long-sleeved pale-blue shirt under his apron.

"Tell 'em what happened," Charlie said.

"Well," Dick said, "It was midnight."

"When?" the detective interrupted.

"Just over four months ago, first day of the month. I'll never forget it."

"So that would be April first?" Tom asked.

"Yeah. We were running low on our house whiskey. It takes less than a minute to grab a couple bottles. I opened the door to the basement and flipped on the light. As I started down, I spotted him."

"Who?" the detective interrupted again.

"The phantom—or at least that's what we called him. Someone wearing a hat ducked behind a stack of boxes. Big fellow too. The light here isn't the best, but I couldn't miss him. Only young folks move that fast."

Dick pointed near the corner of the basement. "That's where he hid."

"How was he dressed?" Kathy asked.

"Hard to say, he wore dark clothes. But I noticed gloves and the hat. In fact, there's his cap," the bartender said, pointing with one arm outstretched. Sure enough, a black baseball hat hung on the wall.

"People don't wear gloves in summertime, either," he added.

The detective's face showed nothing.

Tom asked, "He left his cap behind?"

"Well," Dick continued, "we don't allow customers in the basement. It's off-limits, except for me and Charlie. We keep the door locked. I was halfway down the stairs when I saw the phantom. Frightened me out of my wits—I twisted around and raced back upstairs."

The bartender licked his lips—a nervous habit, thought Kathy. "That guy startled me. Worse, I was sure he *knew* that I had spotted him. We keep a shotgun behind the bar for emergencies. I grabbed it and yelled to the Wyatt brothers—two of our regulars. They sprinted into the basement with me. The Wyatt boys are tough, and I didn't know what I was dealing with. We walked over to that stack. I poked the shotgun out front and nudged the pile, real slow-like." He paused for effect.

"Gone. Just *gone*," Dick murmured. He looked in the distance as seconds passed. "Even the thought of it shakes me." He stopped, scanning their faces and thrusting his hands out in a hopeless gesture. "We checked every inch of this floor. Nothing. He disappeared into thin air."

Dick's voice caught for an instant. "We choked, even the Wyatt boys. At first, they said I was seeing things, but then Ted Wyatt found the baseball cap. It was lying right where you're standing. Next to an empty box. I'll tell you, the whole thing got to me," he concluded, licking his lips once more.

Pete asked, "Did you call the police and report a break-in?"

"Who would believe me? Besides, as far as we could tell, nothing was missing." Silence.

Charlie spoke, breaking the spell. "After the city guys showed up, Dick and I realized what must have happened."

"Yup," Dick said, "it was obvious. When I raced upstairs for the shotgun, the phantom jumped into the tunnel stairs. He lost his cap in the rush. I guess the trapdoor closed behind him. Back then, we didn't figure it out. A secret passageway wouldn't have crossed our minds. Not in a hundred years."

Charlie chuckled again, then pointed to the trapdoor. "But the phantom found it. That's how he got in here. Running into Dick must have been a nasty surprise. So we use a stack of liquor boxes for weight, centered on the false paver," he added with a nervous laugh. "We don't want whoever it was back here. This is primarily a cash business, and we've never had a theft. I'd prefer to keep it that way."

Suzanne glanced over toward Mr. Hearne. "When you turned the basement light on, didn't you notice the false paver was up?"

"Nope," he replied. "A shipment had arrived that morning. Boxes littered the floor. What caught my eye was someone moving in the dim light."

The foursome listened with mounting excitement. Dick had seen the museum thief. *He had almost caught the man.*

Pete walked over and plucked the cap from the hook where it hung. He turned it around in his hands. It was an Arizona Diamondbacks baseball cap. "Size seven and a half," he said. "Your 'phantom' has a big head. I'll bet he wears size-twelve shoes too."

"We've got to get into that tunnel," Suzanne said. "What do you say, Detective Ryan?"

13

ONE AND THE SAME

B uoyed with anticipation, the four mystery searchers awoke early Friday morning, one week since the ghostly adventure had begun. They couldn't wait for ten o'clock. An invitation to join an ongoing police operation—rather than just hearing about it— was still a highly unusual event in their lives.

Pete drove, parking his mother's car on Whiskey Row. Detective Ryan and Bill Holden soon arrived, accompanied by three police technicians.

Charlie Watts, a wide smile on his face, greeted everyone at the bar's front door. "Hey, the crowd's growing! Welcome, come on in, folks. You're getting to be regulars." Then he laughed.

Nine visitors dragged equipment down the stairs and onto the basement floor.

Charlie raised his eyebrows. "Are you guys going to the moon?"

Detective Joe Ryan, Bill Holden, and Rob Pool, a police tech, prepared to explore. Joining them were Tom and Kathy—they had won a draw, much to Suzanne's displeasure. Relief had flooded Pete. *No way* did he want to descend into that dark, close and smelly tunnel.

Everyone helped unpack the aluminum cases.

Suzanne opened the first one. "Hey, these are oxygen tanks!"

"Yup," Bill said. "Each of us requires an emergency air supply. Cave-ins are unpredictable."

"The chances of that are slim, right?" Tom asked.

"You never know," the chief engineer replied, strapping one on his back. "This tunnel is close to a century old, dug by hand, with rotten wooden beams holding up the ceiling. Be prepared, as they say."

Two of the police techs built a makeshift table out of liquor boxes on the basement floor. On top they set up a computer and connected it to a large-screen monitor.

The first concern was safety. That placed the city's chief engineer, Bill Holden, in charge.

"Okay, here's the plan," Bill said. "Rob Pool is the camera operator. Tom and Kathy, you carry the portable lights. Detective Ryan will search for those footprints and any other evidence. I'll follow up behind all of you and keep my eyes on the tunnel's stability. Are you ready to record?" he asked the two techs.

"You bet," one of them replied. "We're live."

The five team members descended into the tunnel, each donning a wireless headset, microphone and safety helmet.

"Everyone set?" There was a murmur of yeses.

"I'll open the escape hatch," Charlie said, enjoying every second of the drama.

He knelt and pressed the corners of the hidden trapdoor. It popped straight up, grinding and squealing to a shuddering halt.

"Be careful of the stairs," Bill advised. His voice—coming out of the headset earphones and his mouth at the same time—created a strange echo effect. "And please stay away from the walls and timbers. We don't want another cave-in."

One by one, the group descended the old wooden stairs. "How's the audio working? Can you hear us okay?" Rob Pool asked.

"Perfect," a tech replied. "Loud and clear. Good image too."

They touched bottom and disappeared into the tunnel. Charlie, Pete, and Suzanne gathered around the video monitor.

"Dirt and dust," Pete said, pointing to the scenes unfolding before them. "And century-old timbers. Look how wide they are. They're big enough to hide behind."

It felt like passing through an eerie time-warp to see where, a century earlier, workmen had cut away the earth and in places even dug down into the bedrock. The camera captured the tunnel's roughhewn walls and hand-chopped ceiling as beams of light bounced like crazy. A layer of dirt stamped with footprints covered the tunnel floor.

Bill halted where the city excavation crew had broken through a few weeks earlier. He pointed straight up a narrow shaft. "Here's where we first entered the passage."

"Okay," Detective Ryan said, pointing downward. "Light up the floor. Let's see what we can find."

Dozens of footprints appeared, clearly visible on the dirt floor.

"Looks as if your excavation boys obliterated the phantom's footprints," the detective said, addressing Bill. "Can't change that. Let's keep going."

Two minutes later they ran into the cave-in. "End of the road," Tom announced.

Back in the Wild West's basement, Suzanne shook her head. "We might be out of luck."

Tom knelt and picked up a handful of dirt at the foot of the cave-in, letting it sift through his fingers. "Dry as a bone," he said.

His comment startled Charlie. "That sure didn't take long."

Pete looked at him, puzzled. "What do you mean?"

"When I went down, the dirt from the collapse was fresh and moist, even though the tunnel itself was dry as a bone. I'll bet the cave-in had occurred a day or two earlier at most."

Suzanne asked, "Did you mention that to Bill Holden?"

"I did," Charlie replied, "and he agreed."

Down below, Kathy noticed one perfect footprint nudged up to the cave-in, pointing east. She aimed her portable light. "Does that look familiar?" she asked.

"Yes, I recognize that imprint," Detective Ryan said. "It's a miracle it survived." He shot a series of still photos. "Get a close-up video, Rob."

Kathy and Tom lit up the footprint as Rob Pool captured a 180-degree view around it. Then the police tech turned the video camera toward Detective Ryan as he measured the print. The detective spoke, almost to himself, his lips moving behind the plastic visor. "Size twelve."

"There's no doubt about it," Kathy said. "The 'ghost' and the 'phantom' are one and the same."

LATER THAT DAY THE FOURSOME MET AT THE SHAKE SHOP, THEIR favorite gathering spot. Prescott's late-afternoon heat was relentless. They ordered ice teas all around—"No sugar for me," Kathy said.

Suzanne led off the meeting. "Charlie Watts was right. When the city excavation crew broke in, the cave-in was recent. He said the earth was still moist."

"But it had dried out when we went down," Tom said.

Pete added things up logically. "Dick said the phantom appeared on April first. We know the tunnel was open, no cave-in. Those footprints proved it. Then the city guys descended on April fifteenth and ran smack into the collapse. There was no getting past it."

"So it was off-limits for the phantom too," Suzanne said.

"Exactly. He wasn't ever coming back."

"When did Roger Holloway spot the ghost?"

Kathy recalled their initial meeting with Dean Wasson. "I wrote May second."

"There you go," Suzanne stated. "A blocked Whiskey Row tunnel means there *has* to be another tunnel."

"You're right," Pete said. "It makes perfect sense. If the thief is gaining access to the museum, he sure isn't coming from Whiskey Row."

"Maybe the secret passage has two legs," Kathy suggested. "The first leg moved the liquor from a nearby safe storage location to the basement of the county courthouse. The second leg transferred the liquor from the courthouse to Whiskey Row."

"Whoa, you might be right," Pete said. "And that storage location must be close by, so they wouldn't have to dig forever—"

"—but far enough away not to alert neighbors or police," Suzanne said, completing his thought.

"I'll bet they delivered the liquor to somebody's garage at night," Kathy said. "How else could they hide the operation?"

Tom's voice rose a notch in volume. "You're onto something! We could check old city maps of downtown Prescott. Whose houses had huge garages?"

The whole team was fired up again.

"Now," Tom continued, "what about the phantom?"

Comments flew around the table.

"His footprint matched the shoe found in the museum," Suzanne said.

Pete said, "A perfect fit."

"It's the same guy!"

"He's big. Wears size-twelve shoes and a seven-and-a-half hat."

"That leaves out Roger Holloway and Jim Bright."

"And Gloria Waldner—obviously!" Kathy said with a giggle.

"We eliminated her as a suspect long ago," Pete said, frowning at his sister.

The noise level rose.

"Hold it," Suzanne said. "Let's take turns."

"Well, here's the thing," Tom suggested. "Whoever the thief is, he's starting out at the other end of the tunnel. He travels from what used to be the liquor warehouse—that's what I'd call it—all the way to the courthouse, right where the two tunnels connect. Find the tunnel, and we'll find him. It's that simple."

Pete doubted it would be that easy. "Simple? That passageway has lain hidden away for close to a century. What are the chances of discovering it now?"

"No one said it would be a slam dunk," Suzanne argued, shooting him a look. "But I agree with Tom."

"Charlie Watts showed us how the trapdoor opens," Kathy said. "I'll bet the museum entrance is identical. And if we're right, somewhere below the museum, the tunnel splits into two branches."

"We need to work fast," Suzanne said. "The thief won't wait long. There's no doubt he's working with a buyer."

Pete agreed. "We scared him off, but he'll be back. Those relics are more than tempting."

"Remember," Kathy said, "Dean Wasson is counting on us."

"What's next?" Suzanne asked.

Tom grinned. "I've got a couple of ideas."

14

SECRET WEAPONS

"The thief knows how to get in," Suzanne explained. "First, he uploads the phony stills—or has a bot do it—in advance, before he even arrives; then he shuts off the alarm system. Once that happens, he can roam the museum without fear."

The foursome had arranged another clandestine meeting with Gloria, early Saturday morning. They needed her approval.

"We'll install a hidden web-enabled laser detector in the entrance area, pointing up the central aisle," Tom explained, dangling the idea in front of her. "When it's activated, an intruder tone will sound on my cell phone. We could beat the 'troublesome creature' at his own game."

"Once that happens, we'll call the police and race over," Suzanne said. "We're only minutes away."

"Make sure you call us too," Kathy said.

"I'll program it to turn on at one in the morning, long after Roger leaves, and off at five a.m.," Tom said.

Gloria liked the idea. "I get it. The thief won't have any clue he's tripped the laser."

"We'll need Ray Huntley's permission," Tom said, encouraged by her response. "He's the president of our school technology club. The hardware will install in minutes. We'll program it off-site."

"Okay," Gloria said. "But I'm getting uncomfortable with leaving Jim Bright out of these conversations. With Dean Wasson away, Jim is my boss. I'm obligated to keep him informed."

"Well, we're still waiting for Detective Ryan to clear Mr. Bright *and* Mr. Holloway," Pete replied.

"But we need their help," Kathy said.

Tom nodded. "Roger has worked the floor for years. He might have seen something. Once we tell him a tunnel exists, it could jog his memory."

Gloria gave in, but concern lined her face. "Okay, I'll keep our secret for the time being. But it leaves me in an awkward position."

Pete understood. "We should hear from Detective Ryan soon."

"There is one other idea we need to consider," Suzanne said.

Tom explained the possibility of electronic GPS trackers. "We can attach one inside each of the two Sinagua relics. If they're stolen, we can track them on my cell phone."

Gloria shook her head. "Neither Dean Wasson nor Jim Bright would approve. These artifacts are rare and fragile. How could you guarantee their safety?"

Tom assured her that there was no danger. "The trackers are small and incredibly light. I can embed them with adhesive tape on the inside floor of each relic. *And* remove them in seconds." He had studied the solution well.

"Just think," Pete said, "if the thief grabs them, we can track both pots. That's huge."

"I get that," Gloria replied, "but it's a decision for Dean Wasson. He's back next week. This has to be his call."

SATURDAY NIGHT, JUST AS ROGER FINISHED WORK, THE FOURSOME sped over to the county courthouse. Their search for the museum tunnel was underway, and the laser hardware was ready to install. The twins pulled up first. Pete and Kathy were right behind them.

"Let's roll." Suzanne's enthusiasm got everyone moving. They had a two-hour window.

"Okay," Tom said. "We gotta be out by two a.m. Let's get it done!"

Pete led the way through the front doors. "Tom, you install the laser hardware. Call me if you need help. We'll tackle the entrance floor. Girls, you take the left side, I'll go right."

"Aye-aye, captain," Kathy said.

Tom found a twelve-foot step-ladder in the storage room and carried it to the entrance. The miniature battery-powered laser fit above the ceiling tiles, aiming directly down at the inside front doors with a field of vision extending ten feet into the museum floor. A narrow scope peeked through a tiny circle cut into the removable tile.

It took only twenty minutes to install the hardware.

"Can you see anything?" Tom asked, jumping off the ladder.

"Nope, nothing."

"It's perfect."

"Good job," Suzanne said.

Tom triggered the laser. A low, ominous *beep-beep* intruder tone pinged out from his cell phone. They all cheered.

Shiny terrazzo slabs with a speckled granite finish graced the museum floor. Each one was a perfect three-by-three-foot square, separated on all sides by thin strips of metal. The four mystery searchers spent the next hour applying pressure on diagonally opposite corners of every slab in the entrance area, employing the formula revealed by Charlie Watts.

"Both sets of opposing corners," Pete instructed. Nothing.

"Try pushing on the top two corners, then the bottom," Tom suggested.

"And the sides, while you're at it," Suzanne said, "every variation you can think of."

"Let's jump on it," Kathy said, half joking.

Still nothing.

"Let's try tapping on every slab," Pete said. "See if we can detect a hollow sound."

They started over again to no avail. There wasn't a noticeable difference from one slab to another.

It was a mystery, no doubt.

"Let's try the walls again," Kathy said.

The walls were trickier. There weren't any sectioned-off panels. "That makes the pressure points impossible to find," Tom said. "Try tapping the walls, listen for a hollow sound."

An hour dragged by. Time was running out as a gloomy level of frustration descended over the foursome.

"Is it possible we were wrong?" Pete wondered.

"We're never wrong," Kathy joked.

"If we *are*, there's no passageway," Suzanne said. "I doubt that very much."

"Me too," Tom agreed. "There has to be a tunnel. We're missing something."

For Suzanne the next step was obvious. "We need Roger Holloway."

WHERE WAS THE THIEF?

Throughout the weekend, Tom's intruder tone failed to trigger. Tension saturated the air as the museum's artifacts remained safe and undisturbed.

On Sunday afternoon, the foursome gathered together for a quick strategy meeting. Any discussion of the thief sent their collective minds reeling.

"I wonder where the heck he is?" Kathy asked. "I mean, at this moment. He's out there somewhere, scheming."

"You know, it's possible we scared him away for good," Pete said, replaying the tackle in his mind. "We might never see him again."

"No way," Suzanne said. "He—or whoever he's working for—is dying to get his hands on those last two relics."

Kathy agreed. "We won't see the end of him until they're gone."

The wait was torturous.

On Monday morning Dean Wasson returned to work. The group had pre-scheduled a meeting for 11:00 a.m.

"Well, well," the dean said as he rose from his desk. He walked to his office door, his hand extended in greeting. "Come in, please. I hear you have a few adventures to share."

The dean, wearing his trademark long-sleeved white shirt and tie, looked tanned and rested. He shook hands with each of the four as they paraded into his office. Gloria followed them in with Detective Ryan right behind her.

To everyone's surprise, Jim Bright strode into the meeting.

"Good to see you again," he said. His piercing blue eyes took in the entire room. Polite conversation reigned for a minute or two.

"Dean Wasson, you look wonderful," Suzanne exclaimed.

"Thank you, I'm working my way back to normal. Welcome, Detective Ryan. Come on in and find a chair. How goes the chase for our troublesome friend?"

"Good morning, sir," the detective replied. "Before we start, I informed Mr. Bright that we have cleared him of any suspicion."

"That was a relief," the assistant director said.

"Wonderful, Jim," Gloria said. "Now we can get you on the 'ghost team.'"

"I'm looking forward to it."

"One other point," Detective Ryan said. "Our discussion today must stay within these walls. If the thief learns what we know, he might disappear. For the sake of the six missing artifacts, we don't want that to happen."

A collective murmured circled the room.

Over the better part of an hour, Dean Wasson and Jim Bright listened in astonishment as the team brought them up to date.

"So we know the ghost has flesh and blood!" the dean said. "The immaterial specter, therefore, is dead." He let out a long, hearty chuckle.

"Not dead, just human," Detective Ryan followed up. "Still active, and perhaps even dangerous."

"Imagine the thief coming in through a tunnel," Jim Bright said. He seemed genuinely shocked.

"At this stage, it's the only possibility left," Suzanne replied. "Since the Whiskey Row tunnel is impassable, the evidence points toward a separate passageway—one that opens into the museum."

"But the entrance has proved elusive," Pete said. "Do either of you have any thoughts? Any unexplained events in past years?"

"Nothing indicating a passageway," Dean Wasson replied, appearing quite perplexed.

"Sorry, not a thing," Mr. Bright said.

The dean expressed wonderment at everything that had taken place since his heart attack. "You have made such progress. I can't thank you enough."

Tom figured it was time to introduce his latest idea. He reached into his jean pockets and pulled out two tiny GPS trackers and set them on Dean Wasson's desk. "We need your permission," he proposed, locking eyes with the dean, "to deploy these."

"What on earth are they?"

"GPS trackers," Tom replied. He picked them up and handed one each to the dean and Mr. Bright. Each tracker—the size of a postage stamp—weighed less than an ounce.

"We want to place them inside the Sinagua artifacts," Suzanne explained, "just in case the thief steals them."

"In which case we can follow them, everywhere they go," Pete said, grinning.

"That's incredible," the dean said, examining the tiny little device in the palm of his hand. "But you must realize our concern is for any damage to the precious artifacts. Wouldn't you agree, Jim?"

"I would," Mr. Bright replied. He held one between two fingers and stared at it intently. "But I can't imagine a threat from this little thing. How would you attach it?"

"Adhesive tape," Kathy replied "Safe and easy. The thief wouldn't have a clue."

"Just assure me that there's no possibility of damage," Dean Wasson reiterated.

Tom promised. "None. Major museums around the world use this technology for all kinds of objects, including many even more precious and fragile than your Sinagua ceramics."

The dean looked at Jim Bright and Gloria once more for assurance. "Okay, let's do it."

The meeting ended. The four said their goodbyes and followed the detective out the front doors. They gathered together for a minute or two.

Tom wondered about Roger Holloway. "Do you expect to clear him soon?"

"Yes," Detective Ryan replied. "But I need another day."

With a start, Pete remembered something. "We forgot to mention the laser beam in the entrance area."

"That's my fault," Tom said. "It never entered my mind."

"Let's leave it alone," Detective Ryan said. "Gloria knows. If she believes it's important, she'll tell the others."

The foursome glanced at him with questioning looks. As usual, the detective's face was a total blank.

Uh-oh, Kathy thought.

15

TRAPPED

At 7:00 a.m. on Tuesday, the boys arrived at the museum. Tom carried a small box of equipment under one arm. The GPS trackers each weighed a fraction of an ounce, and their minuscule batteries lasted for months.

"We can track 'em," Pete said with satisfaction, "no matter how far the pots travel."

The boys walked up to the tall, slender pottery vessels, standing side by side, each on its own pedestal enclosed in Plexiglas. Their elegant designs and muted colors testified to their antiquity.

Pete reached over and gingerly lifted the square-sided enclosure up and over one of the priceless artifacts. He set it down in the aisle, safely out of the way.

Tom said, "It's a good thing both relics have a wide mouth. They're easy to get into." He produced a tiny slip of double-sided adhesive tape and gently pushed it onto the tracker. "Now, I'll place this into the inside bottom of the pot on the side, so it's hard to see... there we go, pushing down... perfect." The operation took all of ten seconds.

Pete asked, "How does someone get it out?"

"Nothing to it," Tom replied. "They can just reach in and tug on the tracker—it'll pop right off. Let's do the next one."

———

A LOW, OMINOUS *BEEP-BEEP* INTRUDER TONE PINGED OUT FROM TOM'S cell phone, waking him from a deep sleep. He leaped out of bed.

It was two fifteen, Wednesday morning.

Tom ran to the door of Suzanne's bedroom. *"Suzie, he's back,"* he whispered in an urgent, hoarse voice. The twins jumped into their clothes and sprinted downstairs. Within two minutes they were in the Chevy, racing out to the museum.

Suzanne touched 911 and reported a thief at Yavapai Courthouse Museum.

The dispatcher's reply shocked them both. "The security company reported it, ma'am. Officers are on the way."

Baffled, the twins glanced at each other.

"What the heck?" Tom scratched his head.

Suzanne figured there was only one answer. "He forgot to turn off the security alarm."

Then she texted Kathy: *He's back.*

Kathy responded seconds later: *See u soon.*

Tom cruised around the front of the courthouse museum. Two police cars, red lights flashing, parked street side with bright headlights illuminating the entrance. Officer Kate Branson stood guard outside. Another police officer walked the building's perimeter.

"Hi, Tom! Hi, Suzanne!" Officer Branson called out in greeting. "There's a lot of action out here this morning."

"Any sign of the thief?" Suzanne asked.

"No, he's long gone. But we discovered where he escaped."

"Escaped? What do you mean?" Tom asked.

"Well, follow me," Officer Branson said, "and I'll show you." They walked over to a window at the far right of the double front doors. Hundreds of tiny pieces of shattered glass crunched under their feet. The huge, jagged opening was large enough for a grown man to squeeze through.

"This is where he got in, right?" Tom asked.

"No," Suzanne replied. "We're standing on the broken glass. It points out, not in. He broke *out* of the museum."

"Exactly," said Officer Branson. "You might make a good detective someday, young lady."

"You're right," Tom said ruefully. He knelt to inspect the glass. "He sure did, no doubt about it."

"Okay," Suzanne said. "In the past, he's always turned off the alarm."

Officer Branson shook her head. "That's different. The security system connects to the motion detectors *and* to the windows, but in a different way. Even with the detectors in off position, the window sensors are active, no matter what, twenty-four/seven. Smash a window, and the alarm triggers an automatic alert. You wouldn't want it any other way. Plus, the fire and burglar alarms ring outside," she added. "That's what happened here. He woke up the entire neighborhood."

Tom poked his head through the broken window, surveying a darkened space. He spotted a metal folding chair lying sideways on the floor. "Hey! The thief used a chair to smash his way out."

"But why?" Suzanne asked.

"The tunnel trapdoor must have closed after he got inside," Tom said. "It wouldn't open again."

"You think it closed by *itself?*"

"Must have. *He* wouldn't have closed it from inside the museum and trapped himself, that's for sure."

Suzanne got it. "I think you're right. We know it doesn't work from inside the museum. We tried pressing on the darn pavers every which way. No matter what we did, nothing budged."

"True enough," Tom said. "Unlike the tunnel entrance on Whiskey Row, this one failed. Somehow, it's defective—at least sometimes."

"The thief found out the hard way."

Just then another sedan pulled up out front with a hard stop. Detective Ryan stepped out of his car and strode over. Suzanne noticed his rumpled suit. *He must sleep in it,* she thought.

"Good morning, Officer Branson," the detective said. He shot a questioning glance to the twins. "I wonder if our friend succeeded this time."

Pete and Kathy arrived next, their eyes flashing with excitement. They shook hands as everyone caught up on the latest news. Right behind them was Gloria, responding to an alarm call from the security company.

"Did he get the artifacts?" she asked, rushing up with a worried frown.

"Doesn't sound like it," Detective Ryan replied. "Open the doors. Let's find out for sure."

Gloria unlocked the front doors and turned on the lights. She walked straight over to the alarm panel. "It's not armed!"

"He disarmed it when he arrived," the detective said, "and left it that way. Why?"

"Because he trapped himself," Pete replied.

"He knew the alarm would go off, armed or unarmed," Suzanne added. "Somehow, he understands the security system really well."

"Right on," the investigator said. "You're way ahead of me."

Kathy played the scene in her mind, picturing the thief hammering the window with a metal chair. "He must have panicked."

"You're not kidding," Tom said.

Everyone followed Gloria as she hurried over to the Sinagua exhibit, passing by the empty and forlorn Hohokam vitrines. The last two Sinagua relics stood safely in position. Nothing had moved.

"Thank you," Gloria said, closing her eyes and breathing a huge sigh of relief.

"He wouldn't have *deliberately* closed the trapdoor, would he?" Kathy asked.

"Not unless he's nuts," Pete replied.

"That's the truth," Detective Ryan agreed. "He was minutes away from stealing the last two Sinagua artifacts. Why bother fooling around with a hundred-year-old mechanism?"

Tom spoke up. "So he found himself trapped inside the museum. That left only one way out."

"The doors are pretty much impossible to break through," Suzanne said. "He had to smash a window to get free."

Gloria brightened with a sudden thought. "Well, there is a silver lining. He might have left us a little gift."

A few minutes later Gloria's office monitor bathed her office with a luminescent glow. First, she downloaded and checked the stills from the interior camera, jumping right to 02:04:00. The group watched, mesmerized once again, waiting for the odd little orb to appear.

"Look!" Gloria exclaimed with a little gasp. There was nothing but empty space in the central aisle. No orb, no thief, nothing. The time code rolled forward without changing color.

"Why?" Kathy asked. "What changed?"

"He knows we're on to him," Tom said. *"That's* what changed. The ghost charade is over. No sense uploading the ghost sequence— it's a thing of the past."

"And a charade from the beginning," Detective Ryan said.

Pete scratched his head. ""The trapdoor must have closed on him as soon as he stepped out, even before he walked into the camera's view."

"But the laser got him," Suzanne said exultantly. "Good job, Tom!"

Tom grinned. "Okay, but what about the outside cameras?"

The two exterior cameras jutted out from the front wall, fourteen feet up, providing a 180-degree, wide-angle view. A set of powerful LED lights cut into the night, illuminating the spacious frontal area.

Gloria downloaded the exterior stills. From the outside vantage point, it was impossible to see an image of the intruder breaking *through* the glass. But soon they spotted a man, frozen in time as he bounded away, legs flying.

"It's the phantom!" Suzanne cried out. "He's even wearing black gloves."

"And a new hat," Kathy said, giggling.

"Darn right." Pete high-fived his sister.

"It's him for sure," Tom said.

"Wow, he's in a big hurry," Gloria said.

"You bet he is," the investigator said. "That burglar alarm is loud. Ever see him before?"

The suspect, his back to the camera and face hidden, wore dark clothing with a matching baseball cap. The still image displayed a man, in sharp detail under the bright lights, tall, with medium-broad shoulders.

"Tough to tell from that shot," Gloria replied. "But he doesn't look familiar."

Detective Ryan said, "Phantom or ghost, that's our thief. And we haven't seen the end of him, either."

The next frame popped up. The man had disappeared into the night.

16

A NEW PARTNER

"There was no reason to suspect *me!*" Roger said, almost shouting. Even in the cool evening and in Gloria's air-conditioned office, sweat poured out of the custodian, staining the shirt over his big belly.

Kathy arched an eyebrow and glanced at her brother and the twins. The man seemed as if he might launch himself into orbit, he was so indignant.

"Look, Roger," Detective Ryan reasoned, "as I've said twice already, you're in the clear. But when a crime occurs, everyone is a suspect. We ran background checks on Dean Wasson, Jim Bright, and even Gloria." He glanced at her as she rolled her eyes. "We treated all of you the same." The investigator leaned forward and locked eyes with the man. "Now calm down and relax."

"We need your help, Roger," Gloria said, reaching over to touch his shoulder. "Without you, we're stuck."

A few minutes passed before the custodian sat back in his chair. His breath heaved out in resignation. Then he listened, asking questions as the group filled him in on the many revelations of the recent days. Pete described his sudden altercation with the thief. Suzanne detailed the amazing discovery of the Whiskey Row tunnel, and Kathy voiced the team's certainty that there was a second tunnel with a hidden entrance—concealed *inside* the museum.

That revelation blew Roger's mind. "You're kidding, right?" Tom's reveal of the laser beam device surprised Roger too.

"Roger, one obvious question we have for you is this," Pete said. "The secret entrance to the tunnel is somewhere inside the museum, near the front doors. It's the only rational place. You know every inch of this building. Have you ever seen evidence of it?"

"I never made the connection," he answered, "but yes, I have."

Glances shot around the room. *Wow.*

"Where? When?" Suzanne asked.

Roger gathered his thoughts. He gripped his suspenders with both hands. "Every so often I come here early in the morning. Real early, around four a.m. I have trouble sleeping, so I stop by and work on minor maintenance projects."

The four mystery searchers, recalling the long, lonely nights on the museum floor, exchanged knowing glances with the same thought: *Good thing we didn't run into him.*

"Well," Roger continued, "one morning I came in to chip away on the inside window frames. Some of them had gotten nicked when we moved in, and it's an easy patch-and-paint job. After I turned on the lights, I walked the floor."

The group hung on to his every word.

"First thing, I noticed a set of footprints that traveled straight up the main aisle. I had left at midnight and returned just four hours later. These old terrazzo slabs were clean as a whistle when I locked up. Mopped the whole floor myself, back to front. Someone had walked around in the middle of the night. Shiny terrazzo shows everything—especially footprints."

"Where did the footprints originate?" Pete asked.

"Well, that's the thing. They started off near the front entrance, just before the *inside* double doors. So whoever it was didn't get in through the main doors. I checked, twice," he added in response to their questioning facial expressions. "My footprints were the only ones coming in from outside. It looked like—like someone had just appeared out of thin air, *inside* the museum."

"How about the emergency door?" Tom asked.

"No footprints there. And if someone had broken in that way, he would've had to walk backward through the whole gallery to leave the prints I found."

"When was this?" Suzanne asked.

"Months ago. Sometime around mid-May."

"Did you call Gloria?" Detective Ryan asked.

"Oh, sure. I called you first thing the next morning," Roger said earnestly, his eyes darting toward the director. "Do you recall?"

"You bet I do," Gloria said. "Worried me half to death. But with no alarm triggered and no obvious signs of intrusion, what could we do? There was no damage, nothing missing. Besides, who could have entered without a key and passcode? It mystified me. All we had was footprints. And frankly—I'm sorry to say this, Roger—I thought you must have been so tired that you somehow mistook your own prints for someone else's. I never even bothered the dean with it. I didn't connect this previous odd incident with the 'ghost.'" She paused. "When I did it was too late."

"Well, one thing is for sure: ghosts don't leave footprints," Roger said with a smile.

It was the first time the foursome had seen the man smile.

"We didn't realize it then," Gloria said, "but it must have been the ghost—I mean, the thief."

"Casing the joint, maybe," said Kathy.

"Or, uh, 'shopping,'" said Pete.

"Then along came May twenty-second," Suzanne said.

"Yup. Believe me, that was a night to remember," Roger said. "The security company woke me. I raced over here and spotted the ghost wandering around the gallery. Freaked me right out."

In his mind, Tom replayed the angry words he had heard on their first visit to the museum. "Roger, do you get along okay with Jim Bright?"

"Oh, so you heard our argument that day?" He cast his eyes

downward. "Jim and I don't get along well. Never have. I accused him of having something to do with the thefts."

"Why?" Detective Ryan asked.

"Over the years he's talked a lot about the value of the Indian artifacts," the custodian replied. "He often said how nice it would be to own one. That night I jogged his memory. He got angry with me and I don't blame him. I was out of line. He loves this museum and its connections. We all do."

The foursome looked at Roger in a new light. They realized he wasn't the person they had thought he was. The museum was his life.

"Can you show us where the footprints started?" Kathy asked.

"Sure. Follow me." The group trailed Roger to the inside double doors.

"They started around here," he said, pointing down toward a spot on the granite floor.

Soon everyone found themselves down on their knees crawling and pressing on the corners of the pavers, including Detective Ryan and Roger... to no avail. Nothing indicated that one of the terrazzo slabs was the entrance to a long-lost tunnel.

But they knew they were close.

"I can almost smell it," Kathy joked.

Later, as Suzanne drove everyone home, Tom sighed, deeply. "We're out of suspects."

"Right," Kathy said. "Detective Ryan has cleared the entire museum staff, which is only four people anyway, and none of them match the thief's profile."

"Which," Pete said, "leaves us with—"

"No one," Suzanne groaned.

17

OPEN SESAME

Everyone involved in the case felt as if a threat was hanging over them. When, they wondered, did the ghost—"the thief," Kathy reminded the team—plan to return? *Or did he?*

"Could be he's sick of the whole game," Suzanne said. "Or all the coverage intimidated him. He knows the police are on the case."

"Well," Kathy reasoned, "he doesn't realize we're on it too."

"The thief is coming back," Tom said. "It's just a matter of time. We have to be ready."

"Agreed," Pete said. "That laser beam will trigger soon enough."

ON FRIDAY MORNING—TWO WEEKS TO THE DAY AFTER THEY HAD started on the case—the four friends returned to Yavapai Court-house Museum. They had scheduled a meeting with Gloria and Jim Bright for 10:00 a.m. in Gloria's office.

"We'd like to try something new," Tom explained. "We can't wait for the entranceway camera you ordered to arrive."

"But we *can* install a high-speed video camera hidden in the ceiling," Suzanne said, "that could show us the exact location of the trapdoor."

"Maybe even who the thief is," Kathy said.

"Thanks to Roger, we know roughly where the thief gets in," Pete said. "It's possible we might capture a clear image of him."

In one fell swoop, they reasoned out loud, the tunnel entrance—together with a sharp image of the intruder—would appear on-screen.

"Plus we can program the camera so that its focus sensor alerts us when it detects a change in its field of view," Tom added, "and we can alert the police. They'll rush over, sirens on, to scare him off—"

"Scare him off?" Jim interrupted. He glanced over at Gloria in surprise

"Why scare him?" Gloria asked, her eyes wider. "Why not capture him?"

"Of course the police will arrest the thief if they can," Tom hurried to reply. "But we think he can dive back into the tunnel faster than they can get to him. And once we know exactly how he gets in—"

"—and where," Kathy finished his thought. "The important thing is to find the entrance and identify the thief... *and* protect your artifacts."

"That makes sense," Mr. Bright said. "Where's the camera going?"

"Above the ceiling tile, like the laser, but just inside the main doors," Tom replied. "Where no one can see it."

"No one? It'll be impossible to spot?"

"Impossible."

IT ONLY TOOK A COUPLE HOURS TO PROGRAM AND TEST THE VIDEO camera at the Jacksons' house. That night, they found a parking space on Whiskey Row, right across the street from the Courthouse Plaza.

Roger was expecting them—the man had become their newest

buddy. Supportive and gung-ho, he was excited to be part of the team.

"He's a whole different person," Tom whispered as they walked up the museum's front doors.

"Nice to have him on our side," Kathy whispered back.

Roger greeted the foursome as they hauled in their box of equipment

"This is the high-speed camera," Tom said.

Suzanne pointed to the floor in the museum, just before the *inside* double doors. "Based on what you told us, we think the thief is getting in somewhere around here."

"We'll place the camera up there," Tom said, pointing to a spot on the ceiling. "I'll aim it back toward the main door and down between the two sets of doors on an angle."

"That will give us the best chance of capturing an image of the thief's face as he emerges from the tunnel," Suzanne added.

"How does the thing work?" Roger asked.

"Well," Pete said, "we've programmed it to capture a still image every ten seconds, just like your cameras."

"Won't the thief hear it?"

"No, it's super quiet."

"The camera is a decent size," Roger said. "Won't he see it?"

"Not to worry," Tom replied. "It goes above the ceiling tiles. Nothing but this special lens peeks out. Look how tiny it is." Tom's enthusiasm was catching. "The camera is Web enabled. We can monitor the stored images remotely on our cell phones. When the thief returns, we'll see where he's coming from."

"Better yet, we'll *see* the guy," Kathy said, pumping one arm in the air.

Roger, the new team player, stroked the back of his neck. "Golly, this is sure to surprise him."

"Well, we're hoping he won't have a clue," Suzanne said. "But you're right. The element of surprise is on our side."

Half an hour later, the team had the camera installed and working. As they ran the final test, Roger peered over Tom's shoulder.

"This is super neat," he said, nodding his head as images filled the screen. "What's next?"

"We wait," Tom replied.

"Tick-tock, tick-tock," Pete teased with a grin.

TOM'S INTRUDER ALARM PINGED AT 2:04 A.M. IN THE MORNING ON Saturday.

The plan quickly unfolded. Tom swung his bare feet onto the bedroom floor as he tapped a preset single-digit emergency code on his cell phone. A text message shot straight to the 911 operator, who Detective Ryan had alerted in advance.

She dispatched a police vehicle from the station, siren on, which was within blocks of the museum.

Everything worked like clockwork.

"Dad, it's happening," Tom called to his father in a soft voice. The Chief jumped out of bed.

"Let's go downstairs," he said.

A minute later the entire family sat at the kitchen table while Tom logged into the app. Suzanne texted an update to Kathy and Pete: *He's back! Pics coming.*

The dispatcher called. As Tom had predicted, the thief had vanished long before Officer Branson had arrived at the museum. "He's gone, Chief. The building is clear. No sign of anyone there. Officer Branson says the exhibits are all still in place."

"Okay, thank you."

"They'll arrive any second," Tom said, nervously waiting for the server to respond. It felt like forever, but a minute later his screen brightened. "Here they come!"

The first shot arrived, and it was stunning.

Suzanne breathed out hard. "Wow. *Open sesame.*"

"There it is," the Chief observed, almost whispering.

Just in front of the inside front doors and off-center to the right, a three-by-three-foot square terrazzo slab was elevated four feet above the floor. The slab seemed to float on four thin iron bars, one at each corner.

Sherri nodded. "You were right."

"We checked that patch of floor so many times!" Tom said.

"For sure," Suzanne agreed. "Notice the lift matches the one in the bar. Same mechanism."

"Makes sense," the Chief said. "I'm sure the same people built both tunnels."

"One works better than the other," Tom said with a grin. He pointed to a four-foot-long chunk of two-by-four lumber jammed into place to prevent the terrazzo slab from dropping.

In the very next frame the camera had captured an image of a tall man with broad shoulders. The figure wore a black bandana wrapped tightly round his face and a ball cap pulled low. He faced away from the camera, looking up to the ceiling.

"Wow, there he is!" Sherri's hand flew to her mouth.

"Darn it," Tom exclaimed with a frown. "We didn't get a clean face shot."

"Awfully difficult with that bandana and visor, and facing away from the camera," Suzanne remarked.

"Why is he looking up at the ceiling?" Tom puzzled. He clicked to the next frame. The phantom had disappeared, and the trapdoor was closed.

The Chief leaned closer. "He sure didn't spend much time in there. Not even half a minute. Your plan worked." Then he sat back, running his fingers through his hair.

"Forward those to Detective Ryan," the Chief said.

"Done," said Tom.

18

A SECRET BUG

The next morning, a mounting sense of excitement filled the Jackson and Brunelli team. Overcoming a serious lack of sleep, the four friends arrived at the museum, right behind Gloria.

Roger struggled in next. Despite complaining about how early it was, he loved being included—and it showed. Jim Bright followed Detective Ryan.

"Well, we got half of what we wanted," the investigator grumbled, disappointed that there wasn't an identifying image of the thief. Still, a look of satisfaction crossed his face—the case had taken another promising new turn.

The four friends were on their knees, searching for the three-by-three-foot pop-up trapdoor.

Tom checked the image on his intruder app for the umpteenth time. "Not that one. *This one.*"

"We're much smarter than the thief," Kathy said as she touched the barely palpable, slightly raised edge of the trapdoor. The still image had given away the secret entrance.

Roger found a piece of chalk. Suzanne drew an outline on the floor.

"We only walked over it about a hundred times," she said.

"That's okay," Roger said, chortling. "I've walked it thousands of times and never had a clue."

"Not surprising at all," Jim Bright said. "Just think. It sat here without moving for darn near a century."

"Press the corners and see if moves," Gloria suggested. To no one's surprise, the trapdoor refused to budge.

"We'd jump a foot if it did," Kathy quipped.

"Okay," the detective said, surveying the group. "Thanks to all of you, we found it. Now we have choices. One, we can break through this floor and follow the tunnel to where it begins. But I'd prefer not to."

"Why not?" Tom asked.

"We don't know the thief's identity. We could rush out at the other end of that tunnel to find he's not home."

"Or that he's armed, or has accomplices," Pete said, picking up the detective's line of reasoning. "That makes sense."

"In either case he might pull a vanishing act," Detective Ryan continued. "And we'd never locate the missing relics. The second choice is—"

"To catch him in the act!" Kathy crowed triumphantly.

"Or if we miss him by minutes," Suzanne said, "*then* we smash the floor in and chase him."

Tom was thinking ahead. "Someone needs to greet the thief on his next visit."

"Oh, let's not *greet* him," Pete said, holding his hands up and pointing to the crown of his head. "I did that already."

"But he took you by surprise," the detective said. "This time is different. I agree we arrange a welcoming committee. Its sole purpose would be to summon reinforcements."

Suzanne locked eyes with her best friend. "We could do it."

"Yes, we volunteer," Kathy said.

"Could he know about the camera?" Roger asked. "Is that why he's wearing a bandana?"

"Only if there was a leak," Pete replied.

"Oh, brother, here we go again," Gloria spoke up with a groan.

"We're not sure of anything," the detective counseled.

Jim Bright turned defensive. "Let's not jump to conclusions. No one here has shared information outside the investigating team. There must be another reason."

They all agreed a reception committee would go a long way to catching the thief.

"I'm all for it," the investigator said, putting his stamp of approval on the plan. "Just remember our purpose: if the thief appears, you keep your head down and summon reinforcements. No more improvised nosediving at his legs. Nothing else, right?"

Soon enough everyone went their separate ways, except for the twins, who hung around for a few more minutes.

"I want to check something out," Tom said quietly to his sister.

"What is it?"

"Well, here's the shot of the intruder," Tom said, bringing the image up on his cell phone. "Notice he's looking straight up at the ceiling. What the heck is up there?"

The two of them stood near the trapdoor paver, their eyes searching the ceiling panels.

"I don't see anything," Tom said.

"Let me try," Suzanne said. She moved a few inches closer. Nothing. She changed her angle of view and stepped back a foot. A tiny glint of light sparkled back at her. Suzanne pointed.

Tom brought his face close to his sister's and caught the glint. Something shiny was peeking out from a corner tile, glittering down at them. It was the size of a pinky fingernail.

Don't talk, Tom whispered to his sister. He ran off and returned with a ladder, propping it up under the shiny object. He climbed up and gently pushed a tile to one side.

There he uncovered a tiny microphone attached to a small metal box—a one-inch cube—taped to the structure above the tile. It was a first for Tom: the box, he realized, was a battery-operated bug. A transmitter. *Wow.*

Suzanne watched intently from the floor below.

Tom slid the tile back into place and stepped down. He put a finger to his lips before carting off the ladder.

"It's a microphone, and I left it live," Tom said in a quiet voice once they were well away from the device. "That thief is a *serious* high-tech guy."

A light went on in Suzanne's mind. "So there wasn't a leak, after all."

"Well, there was a *technology* leak," Tom replied. "My guess is that bug broadcasts for a few blocks at most. The thief can listen in any time he feels like it… but he has to be in range."

"He heard us looking for the tunnel. He listened in on us."

"Yup. And when we installed the camera too. That explains the bandana."

"Talk about a high-tech guy."

"Somehow, he *didn't* hear us install the laser beam," Tom added. "He was obviously out of range that day. Let's hope he missed the conversation this morning too."

The twins sent messages to everyone whose phone number they had—the Brunellis, Dean Wasson, Gloria, Jim Bright, the Chief, and Detective Ryan: *Caution: The thief bugged the museum entrance. Don't talk about the case anywhere around the inside front doors!*

19

DISCOVERY

Pete and Kathy lay hidden in the first display—after midnight, early on Monday morning—a few yards past the inside double doors. Every so often, out of pure boredom, one them glanced around the corner. They had a clear, straight line of sight to the tunnel's trapdoor.

"Nothing—for the umpteenth time," Kathy murmured. She sat back, leaning against a short, paneled wall, all but invisible, scanning an article about her favorite Broadway star. Her cellphone flashlight came in handy.

Pete sighed, not tired in the slightest. He had spent an hour leafing through old copies of *Mechanix Illustrated* by the light of a headlamp. His dream was to go into engineering right out of high school. Later he switched over to his favorite classic, *Moby Dick,* which he was reading for the third time.

At 1:00 a.m., Tom called out, "You still awake?"

"That's the plan," Kathy replied.

"Reassuring."

"Think he'll show?"

Suzanne answered. "The sooner, the better. This is getting old."

The mystery searchers had flipped a coin to decide where each team would hide. Pete and Kathy won and chose the front of the museum. The twins moved to the back, across the aisle from the Sinagua exhibit.

The wind picked up, forcing tree branches to scrape eerily against the granite exterior walls. Then it faded to a stillness that descended onto the courthouse.

"Sure is spooky!" Kathy said, raising her voice.

"A century-old building and a mysterious, ghostlike intruder," Suzanne replied. "Plus it's the middle of the night. Spooky is the right word."

Another hour passed before Kathy drifted into sleep. Pete yawned. It was 2:25 a.m. *A no-show for sure*, he thought. *Time to relax.* He switched off his reading light and stretched out onto the floor. "Hey, you guys still awake?" he called out to the twins. No reply.

Just as he lay his head down, the grinding sound began. The hairs stood up on the back of his neck. Adrenaline flowed through his veins. He grabbed Kathy's arm and shook her awake, warning her with a finger over his mouth. They sat up and peeked around the corner of the display wall, transfixed as the terrazzo slab rose, squealing to its maximum height. It shuddered, halting in midair. The thief ducked out from beneath the floor. A black bandana covered his face, and a ball cap was pulled low over his forehead.

He pivoted toward the alarm box. *He's shutting it down, Kathy* figured. They knew the new camera was busy capturing images. *Were the twins awake?*

To the siblings' shock, a second man appeared. Shorter and heavier, he moved like an older person with an awkward gait. A black bandana covered his face too. He stood in the central aisle for a moment, waiting. "Move it."

"The alarm's already off!"

"*So what.* Let's go."

Then the siblings heard a spraying sound that lasted a few seconds. They glanced at each other. *What's that?*

The two men hustled down the aisle.

Pete and Kathy shrank back as they passed, just inches away.

Then they grabbed their cell phones and slipped into the aisle, crouching low and duck-walking on tiptoe over to the trapdoor. Moonlight fell across the opening in the floor, illuminating a set of stairs below that faded into darkness. Jammed into the trapdoor was a four-foot length of a two-by-four.

Oh, man, that's scary. Pete looked down into the tunnel. He swallowed hard and turned away, just for a second. A choking feeling engulfed him, but he knew he had to beat the awful sensation that attacked him in close quarters. Solving the case depended on it.

Pete caught his sister's eye and mouthed something, but Kathy didn't get it. He pointed down and forced himself onto the stairs, walking on his toes down one side of the steps, trying to be as silent as possible. At the bottom he stepped onto a solid dirt floor and turned around, happy to see Kathy right behind him.

"Are you nuts?" she hissed in his face. "You realize how much trouble we'll be in?"

"We'll follow these guys."

"You *are* nuts!"

They clicked on their cell phone flashlights to find themselves at a fork: two wide tunnels stretched out before them, left and right. A thought flashed through Kathy's brain: *We were right!*

Pete beamed light to their left. "The Whiskey Row tunnel," he muttered, picturing the layout of the streets above them. The second tunnel veered right, off into the distance. It was obvious: the intruders *had* to head right.

The siblings hurried left, confident the men wouldn't follow, hiking a short distance before spotting one of the century-old timbers. They crouched on its far side. Pete worked hard to control his breathing. *This isn't so bad.*

Kathy texted Suzanne. *Don't call for help! We're in the tunnel. See what happens.*

Suzanne had muted her cell phone and fallen asleep with the device by her ear. The vibrating incoming message woke her. She scanned it and shook Tom. He awoke with a start and spotted the intruder alerts. The camera and the laser had detected an incursion. *What's going on?*

A rustling noise. As the twins peered out, a man carted something past their hiding place. He wore a black bandana. *The thief.*

Not one thief, but two! The big guy's arms grasped one of the Sinagua pots. A shorter man followed behind, carrying the second relic. He was older, limping, but still moving quickly.

The twins half stood for a better view as the men rushed down the gallery's central aisle toward the entranceway. Tom and Suzanne glided up the aisle, desperately trying not to make a sound. *Too late!* From out of the dark void below, they watched an arm reach up to yank out a length of wood. Then the terrazzo panel sank into the museum floor down with its weird grinding noise and a final *clunk.*

Hopelessness washed over the twins. Their hearts sunk. What about Pete and Kathy? *What the heck?*

Suzanne's cell phone vibrated again. "Whew." Another text arrived. *Hang on, we're coming for you.*

The twins froze, unsure what to do next. Two minutes crept past. It seemed like an eternity before the trapdoor squealed up and the lift halted in midair.

"Come on in," Pete said, his voice hushed. He clicked his light twice.

"Yeah, before the darn thing drops on you," Kathy whispered.

"Wh-what on earth are you two doing?" Suzanne said, stammering.

"*Shh.* Get down here and we'll show you."

Tom counted twelve steps to the bottom with Suzanne right behind him.

"Keep your voices down," Pete counseled. "They're not too far in front of us."

"What do you mean 'in front of us?'" Tom asked. "You're not thinking we'll follow them?"

"Are you kidding? Of course we will."

Suzanne couldn't believe her own ears. "You realize what are our parents will say—what my dad will *do?*"

"It's worth it. We're about to solve a major crime. That's what mystery searchers do."

"I couldn't talk him out of it," Kathy said in her own defense. In the darkness, she rolled her eyes to herself.

"This tunnel is dangerous," Tom reminded. "It's already collapsed once!"

"Maybe. But these guys have been running around in it for weeks," Pete replied. "We'll be fine."

Tom held his cell phone out. He had only to dial the preset emergency code to summon an army. "We can get help."

"Oh, sure. I know that. But first, let's check things out."

A hushed argument raged on for another minute before they reached a compromise.

"Okay. We'll follow these guys, but nothing more," Tom said. "This is risky."

"We'll be careful," Pete chortled.

Cell phone flashlights clicked on, beams bouncing off walls as Pete explained about the two tunnels in a hushed tone. "The left one is the route to Whiskey Row. The two thieves went right."

"Oh, boy, were we right!" Suzanne said.

"It's so wide… and high," Kathy said, overcome by a sense of awe. The museum tunnel appeared larger than the Whiskey Row tunnel. A musty smell permeated the air. The dust at their feet was dry as bone.

Pete cupped his cell phone, allowing minimal rays to filter through his fingers.

"Enough to see where we're going," he said. "We don't want to alert them."

"You've got that right," Tom replied. He swallowed hard and clicked off his flashlight. The girls followed suit.

The mystery searchers trekked along the museum tunnel, trying to make little noise and pausing every few moments to listen. "Dead quiet," Suzanne whispered.

"Very," Kathy replied, comforted by the sound of her own voice.

It was difficult to judge distance, but they guessed they had hiked a city block. The tunnel appeared to run in a straight line.

Soon enough, a second set of stairs loomed ahead, bathed in soft blue light that receded in the depths. They came to a dead stop. Pete turned off his flashlight. Low voices drifted toward them along the tunnel walls.

"The trapdoor is open," Kathy whispered tensely.

"I'll peek," Pete said.

"Be careful," Suzanne hissed. "I can hear them."

Pete started up, again keeping both feet at the outside edges of the old wooden stairs and walking on his tiptoes, as silent as possible.

Without warning the trapdoor sank down into the floor with a grinding squeal. Pete drew back as the blue light yielded to pitch black. A solid *click* snapped the trapdoor flush into place.

"Crap," Pete whispered. "We missed them by seconds."

"We missed being *captured* by seconds," Suzanne retorted, turning on her phone flashlight. "That was lucky. What now?"

"It's the middle of the night," Pete said. "They won't hang around for long. Let's give them thirty minutes. Then we'll open the trapdoor and see what's up top."

"We're in for it if they're still there," Kathy warned.

"They won't be," Pete said. "You can count on it. Otherwise—"

"—we're dead," Suzanne finished.

"Chill."

Minutes crawled by as the foursome rested on the tunnel floor, well back from the stairs. They talked in quiet tones, discussing the case and everything that had led them to where they were.

"You realize dad will ground us for the rest of our lives," Kathy declared, poking her brother in the side.

Pete was running on pure adrenaline. He couldn't wait. "Are you serious? We're about to solve a major case and save the museum. We'll be famous!"

"Good luck with that."

"Whose basement is up there?" Tom wondered out loud.

"We'll soon know," Suzanne said.

"*Ten... nine... eight...*" Kathy counted off the last few seconds. Then Pete slipped up the steps and put his ear up to the trapdoor. Nothing.

"Okay," he said. He paused, taking sharp breaths. This was it: no turning back. "I'm going for it."

Tom's finger rested on his phone, ready to dial his father's emergency code.

Pete reached out and grabbed the curved, black metal handle. He pulled on it once. The trapdoor started up with a variant on its grinding noise, but no squeal. It opened into utter darkness. He poked his head up into... *what?*

"Gone."

"Darn good thing."

The three others followed, sprinting up and out onto a cement floor. "Where *are* we?" Suzanne asked.

Four cell phone flashlights clicked on, shooting random beams of light every which way. Instead of someone's basement, they had entered an immense, enclosed pitch-dark space. High above was a barely discernable ceiling, but in every other direction their lights faded into darkness. Wherever they were, the area was so large they couldn't even see walls.

They threaded their way in silence around boxes and crates of every size and shape.

Pete muttered to himself. "What the heck is this place?"

A windowless, twenty-foot-high wall loomed before them. Hundreds of stackable chairs and long folding tables rested against its base. They strode alongside it for another three hundred feet before running into an adjoining wall.

Tom let out a low whistle. "This is bigger than our school auditorium. It's *gigantic*."

They passed dozens of vast painted sheets of canvas hanging from iron pipes, attached by wires to some structure high in the ceiling. Kathy paused, thinking the one in front looked vaguely familiar. She ran a beam of light over it. Seconds slipped past before it registered.

"Look! I recognize this! *I know where we are.*"

"You're kidding. What is it? Where are we?"

Kathy backed away and cast her light across the entire backdrop. "It's *The Phantom of the Opera!*"

Pete stifled a laugh. "What on earth are you talking about?"

"It's from the musical, remember? We were here a few weeks ago."

"Wow, you're right!" Tom said. "This is the backdrop for the closing scene. We—"

"We were wrong. The entrance to the tunnel isn't in someone's house," Pete said, projecting his flashlight toward his best friend's face. "We're in the basement of the Opera House!"

Suzanne stiffened. "*Shh.* I hear something."

20

POETIC JUSTICE

An overhead set of fluorescent lights buzzed. In a heartbeat the foursome pivoted, racing for the trapdoor at top speed. The light sets flickered on in a wave, one bank after another.

Kathy reached the opening first and darted down the stairs. Pete rushed behind her, landing hard on his left foot. He stumbled as pain shot up his leg.

"Are you okay?" his sister asked.

The twins were right behind them, with Tom last into the tunnel. He yanked the black handle as he whipped past it.

"Hey!" a voice shouted. *"Hey!"*

The trapdoor slipped down into the floor, and the soft blue light faded.

"Let's go!" Tom shouted in an adrenalin rush. The need to whisper was long past. Whoever yelled at them knew *exactly* where they were. Suzanne sped forward.

Pete held back but hurried as fast as possible.

"What's the matter?" Tom asked. He halted and turned around.

"He hurt his foot coming off the stairs," Kathy shouted as she grasped her brother's arm.

"I can still make it."

Tom flipped back and grabbed his other arm. "I'll help you."

Suzanne touched the emergency code programmed into her phone. "Uh-oh. No signal underground."

"That's not good," Kathy said. In the distance behind them a glow appeared. "We've got to move fast. *They're coming.*"

Pete hobbled along, but it was slow going. "Go on without me... get help."

"No way," Tom said. "We're in this together."

Moving in tandem was difficult. The ominous sound of footsteps pounded toward them, closer now.

"You guys better escape while you can."

"No! Just keep going."

"Stop!" someone yelled. "Hold up where you are!"

"Ignore them," Suzanne said in a rasping voice.

Pete struggled to maintain the pace. "It's my ankle. I must have sprained it."

A gunshot! They heard the bullet whiz by their ears, ducked down but kept going, struggling to move faster. *Another shot!*

Without warning, the sound of a mighty roar filled the tunnel. It felt like it lasted forever. Then, there was an unexpected scream of pain!

They came to an abrupt halt and turned their flashlights behind them. In a heartbeat, a vast cloud of swirling brown dust hammered them, engulfing the tunnel from top to bottom, wall to wall. For a few moments they lost sight of one another, but as fast as it materialized the brown cloud blasted past them, disappearing into the darkness ahead. They bent over, hacking and coughing in a haze.

Silence and stillness filled the void as Suzanne straightened and looked about her. "Who screamed?"

"The tunnel collapsed," Tom said, his voice raspy. He coughed again. His finger searched for the emergency code. Still no signal.

The pungent smell of musty dirt flooded their nostrils. A layer of fine brown dust seemed to penetrate every pore of their skin.

Pete's throat was dry, his eyes watered. "The gunshots must have triggered a cave-in."

"*Help!*" a voice pleaded. "Please... help me."

"Could be a ploy," Kathy said, worried.

"Help..." the voice called again. This time weaker.

"That's no ploy," Tom said. "Someone's in big trouble."

They stepped back, cautiously, Pete limping all the way. There wasn't far to go.

Their flashlights' beams revealed the shocking damage. On the floor of the tunnel, a huge timber emerged from a heap of dirt seven feet high. What had once been a ceiling was gone. Under it all lay a man, trapped beneath the heavy timber, buried up to his neck, his face severely gashed, arms stretched out in front. Pinned to the ground.

Kathy stopped, stunned as she moved closer. She bent over to examine the man's face. "It's Philip!" she cried aloud.

"Philip who?" Pete demanded.

"Philip Woodson, the audio technician from the Opera House."

"Th-thank God," the man whispered. "I'm hurt bad."

They knelt to help the young man.

Tom took one look at his huge hands. "You're the phantom, aren't you?"

There was no response. His eyes closed as he slipped into unconsciousness.

Pete felt for pulse. "Oh, man, this sucks. I don't know if he'll make it."

"So here's the phantom of the opera," Kathy said, "in the cellar beneath the Opera House, his face disfigured. Sound familiar?"

Tom examined the thief's bloody face, now turned a ghastly gray. "He's sure in rough shape. Let's try to pull this timber off him."

The tall century-old support—two feet square, solid as stone and crushed by the weight of the collapsed dirt—refused to budge.

"It's dead weight," Suzanne said, shaking her head after tugging and pulling the timber. "No way can we move it."

"He's unconscious," Pete said. "He must have broken bones too. You'd better go for help. I'll stay here."

"I guess you're right," Tom said, somewhat reluctant. The thought of calling his father now seemed... well, *daunting*. "What happened to the older man?"

"Someone was shooting at us. I don't see a gun here."

"Maybe it's buried under the other guy."

"Oh, man, I hope not." Tom stood up, tracing a beam over the cave-in. "You sure you'll be okay, Pete?"

"I'm staying with him," Kathy said in a firm voice.

"Go!" Pete shouted.

"Okay," Tom said. "We're out of here."

The twins ran back up the tunnel. Two minutes later they leaped up the steps into the museum. Tom touched his emergency code at the same time.

SOON, THE COUNTY COURTHOUSE RESEMBLED A WAR ZONE. POLICE cars, fire engines, ambulances, and city vehicles parked randomly around the famous old structure. Two television trucks had pulled up front. Heidi Hoover wasn't far behind.

Detective Ryan showed up in his rumpled suit. The anxious Jackson and Brunelli parents descended on the museum at the same time.

"Whose idea was this?" the Chief asked his twins, furious that they had put themselves in such danger—and that someone had taken potshots at them.

"We all went for it, Dad."

"I'd call this reckless and irresponsible. You could all have gotten yourselves killed. We'll discuss this later."

But their mother provided big hugs. "You're okay now, that's what counts."

Soon, the Brunelli siblings emerged from the tunnel with Pete resting on a gurney surrounded by four paramedics.

"Hi, everybody," he called out. "I'm fine. Just a little sprain."

Joe and Maria showed their relief. Maria gave her impetuous son a big hug, but Joe wasn't quite as forgiving. "I've told you this before. You need to think before you act."

Seconds later, Pete was on the way to Prescott Regional Medical Center for an X-ray.

An argument ensued between city officials and the paramedics.

"You can't move dirt and timbers around that tunnel without safety equipment," Bill Holden contended.

"No choice," the fire chief replied. "That fellow will die unless we get him out fast. He might be dead already."

The two hundred-pound timber was no match for a team of firefighters armed with shovels. Soon the unconscious phantom was heading to the same hospital as Pete, but not before Detective Ryan had grabbed a close-up photo.

The three remaining mystery searchers had one more concern. The Chief, Detective Ryan, Bill Holden, and the city's fire chief surrounded them, listening with rapt attention.

"So it's possible there's another man under the dirt," Tom concluded. "Or the cave-in might've just missed him, and he headed back into the Opera House."

"We'd better work fast," the fire chief said. "If there is someone else buried in that cave-in, he's in serious trouble. Do either of you know how to access the tunnel from the Opera House?"

The twins exchanged glances. "We think so," Suzanne replied, "but I can't guarantee it'll open the same way."

"That's okay," the fire chief replied. "We'll smash in if necessary. Let's go."

"How do we get into the building?" Tom asked.

The Chief thought of Bob Carlson, his old high school friend and the executive director of the Opera House. Kathy recalled the friendly stage manager, Robert Burns.

"You try Mr. Burns," the Chief said. "I'll take Bob Carlson. Both will have keys." Information provided phone numbers; Burns was the first to answer. Kathy handed her cell phone to the fire chief. It was three thirty in the morning.

Prescott's fire chief explained the emergency. "Every second counts. How soon can you get here?"

"Ten minutes," Robert Burns answered.

"Too late. We'll smash a door and go in."

21

NOT ONE, BUT TWO

A stream of vehicles raced to the Opera House. Kathy rode with the detective, while the twins hopped into the fire chief's car.

Emergency personnel followed Tom into the basement. The fluorescent lights cascaded on once more. Tom circled around hundreds of boxes and crates.

"It's about here. Give me a hand, girls."

The three threw themselves on the floor, pushing the corners of the surrounding pavers.

A minute later, Suzanne jumped up and whooped. "Stand back, everyone!"

With its trademark strange mechanical groan, the trapdoor popped up, rising to its maximum height and shuddering to a halt.

"You go, girl!" Kathy shouted, giving her best friend a high-five.

A team of paramedics rushed into the tunnel. Two minutes later, they called for shovels.

"Not a good sign," the Chief muttered.

At that moment Robert Burns hurried into the basement. He peeked beneath the trapdoor. "What the heck is *that?*"

The three mystery searchers shook hands with the stage

manager. They filled him in on the startling early morning events and introduced him to everyone else.

"Hello, Mr. Burns," Detective Ryan said. "I wonder if you can help us."

"I'll try."

The detective pulled out his cell phone. He displayed a picture of the unconscious spook, taken as paramedics lifted the man out of the tunnel. "Do you recognize him?"

Shocked, Robert confirmed what the investigator already knew. "Oh, yes, I sure do. That's Philip Woodson. He's our head audio technician. Is he okay?"

"He got caught in the cave-in," the detective replied. "They think he'll pull through, but he's in rough shape."

"We spotted a second man," Tom said. "An older fellow, shorter and heavier. He had an awkward gait."

"Oh, sure," Robert said. It was obvious he wanted to help. "Guy Davidson is the musical director of the Opera House. He hurt himself in a car accident years ago. He limps."

"Are Philip Woodson and Guy Davidson close friends?" the Chief asked.

"You bet," Robert said. "Thick as thieves."

At that moment, paramedics emerged from the tunnel, easing a stretcher up the stairs and under the trapdoor. On it was an unconscious man, securely strapped into place.

"Make way!" the fire chief called out, clearing a path. "This guy's in bad shape."

As the gurney passed by, Detective Ryan snapped a photograph of the man's face with his phone.

"Oh, my goodness," Robert said. "That's Guy. What on earth is going on?"

Suzanne realized no one had called Gloria. Although she woke the groggy museum director up at four in the morning, Gloria rushed into the basement just fifteen minutes later. A large group of people filled her in on the morning's shocking events.

"Do you recognize this young man?" the detective asked, displaying the phantom's face shot.

"Well," she replied, holding a hand to her mouth, "he *looks* like one of the installers of our security system. I haven't seen him since, and I don't know his name. What's the matter with him? He doesn't look too good."

Detective Ryan stared hard at Gloria. "How come you never mentioned this guy before now?"

"He never crossed my mind," she replied nervously. "I haven't laid eyes on the man in over a year. Is he important to the case?"

"Oh, my gosh," Suzanne exclaimed. "No wonder he was able to hack into their system. He helped set it up!"

LATER, AS DAWN BROKE OVER PRESCOTT, THE OPERA HOUSE EMPTIED. People headed home or back to work. The city employees, fire chief, and paramedics left, one after the other. The television and newspaper reporters melted away too, including Heidi Hoover.

Gloria talked with the Chief and Detective Ryan.

"I was so relieved when the twins found the bug. That took away any suspicion of my coworkers."

"Yes, very helpful," the investigator replied. "The technician who installed that microphone is in the hospital. He won't be bothering us any longer."

Tom wandered around the basement of the Opera House, his face buried in his cell phone. The tracker app displayed a blinking icon only yards from where he stood. A second icon sat stationary, not five miles away.

"I found a relic," he yelled, overjoyed that his technology was proving its worth. He zeroed in on a giant red crate. "This explains why they came back in the middle of the night."

Detective Ryan leaned toward the crate. "It's got a huge padlock on it."

Minutes passed before they found a cutter. The lock fell onto the floor with a bang and Tom swung the top open. One of the missing Sinagua pots lay nested in a dense nest of bubble wrap and packing peanuts.

Suzanne let out a loud whoop.

"Wonderful," Gloria exclaimed. "Where's the other one?"

With a little help from Tom's technology solution, police located the second priceless artifact in a drive-in storage locker on the edge of town. Twenty minutes later, they seized it for evidence.

EARLY THE NEXT MORNING, THE FRONT-PAGE HEADLINE OF *THE DAILY Pilot* blazed out: "The Ghost in Yavapai County Courthouse!" A subhead read: "Two men arrested." The dramatic story unfolded, complete with an executive-portrait-type head-and-shoulders shot of the well-known Mr. Davidson:

A mysterious ghost haunted Yavapai Courthouse Museum for the past few weeks. At the same time, six of the museum's famous Indian artifacts disappeared. It turned out there were two "ghosts." Yesterday, Prescott City Police formally charged Guy Davidson, forty-three years old, the musical director of Prescott's Opera House, with a litany of charges, including multiple counts of grand theft and four counts of attempted murder. City officials expressed shock at the news.

His accomplice, Philip Woodson, twenty-three years of age, was similarly charged. Both men, badly injured in the collapse of a Prohibition-era underground tunnel, are in serious but recovering condition at Prescott Regional Medical Center.

A third person, Pete Brunelli, sustained a slight injury while escaping from the two suspects through a long-abandoned tunnel system that connects the Opera House to Yavapai County Courthouse and Whiskey Row. Mr. Brunelli and his team of mystery searchers broke the case wide open by tracking the thieves to the Opera House through the hidden underground tunnel.

The four young people who solved the case are well known to readers of The Daily Pilot. Earlier this summer, they took on the mystery on Apache Canyon Drive, breaking up a major counterfeiting operation and returning a lost child to her mother.

THE ADVENTURE OF THE GHOST IN THE COUNTY COURTHOUSE WAS over.

Almost.

22

THE MYSTERY REVEALED

"Guy Davidson is all lawyered up," Detective Ryan said in his trademark drawl. He had called early in the morning, two days later. "He won't talk to us, but last night I had a long visit with Philip Woodson. He wants the four of you to visit him, but he specifically asked for Kathy."

"Oh, wow," Suzanne replied. "She interned at the Opera House, and that's where they met. I'll let everyone know. Is he okay?"

"He'll live, but he's beat up pretty bad. His face will need plastic surgery and his left leg is broken. Lots of other cuts and bruises. But he's got quite a story to tell."

An hour later the foursome pulled up to Prescott Regional Medical Center. They headed in through the emergency center.

The Brunellis' mother, Maria, met them in the waiting room. "Philip is in the recovery center on the fifth floor, room 545. He's in rough shape, but a very lucky young man considering what landed on him. His broken leg is held together with pins, screws, and a metal plate."

"*Eww,*" Kathy exclaimed, drawing up her face. "The poor guy."

Two minutes later, they walked into Philip Woodson's darkened room. He lay in bed, bandaged from head to toe. One leg was elevated, and a brace supported his neck. His eyes peered out between bandages.

"Hi, Philip, it's Kathy."

"H-Hi, Kathy," he stammered. His head tilted slightly toward them. "I appreciate you coming. I-I wanted to thank you for saving my life."

"Oh, Philip, we're just happy you'll be okay," she replied, holding back tears. *He looks awful.* She introduced her brother and the twins.

"We met you the night of the musical," Suzanne reminded him, "at the Phantom of the Opera."

"Oh, sure, I remember you." He hesitated for a few seconds. "You know, I didn't fire my revolver at you. I fired one bullet into the ceiling, that's all."

"Well, thanks for that!" Suzanne exclaimed. "Is that what triggered the cave-in?"

"Probably," Philip replied. "I swear it happened a second later."

"One thing we never figured out," Pete said, "is how you discovered the tunnel in the first place."

"By accident."

"Seriously? How?" Kathy asked, her eyes widening. "How did you find it?"

"I was working late one night. A heavy box rested on one corner of the trapdoor paver and I stepped on the other corner. The trapdoor popped up about an inch. Blew me away. I pulled the box aside and the trapdoor opened all the way up. So I went exploring."

"Was that just before the first of May?" Kathy asked.

"Yes, it was," Philip replied. "The next day I took Guy Davidson for a walk. When we discovered the museum opening, he realized it was a super opportunity to get rich."

Just then a nurse walked into the room. Everyone stood back while she took the young man's vitals and checked his meds. As she adjusted his elevated leg, Philip grunted with pain. The nurse slipped into the hallway.

Tom asked, "So it *was* you in the basement of the bar."

"Yes," Philip replied. "The bartender surprised me, but I got away."

"Why the ghost plan?"

"That was Guy's crazy idea." Philip turned a little to the side, catching his breath as he moved. "Just to throw the police off track while he sold the artifacts. I told him that I had all the museum's log-in info for the Cloud. So Guy had me shoot video of the museum floor. Then I created the 'ghost' sequence and uploaded it each time I came."

"When you arrived in the museum?"

"No, before I came. It was a simple upload, the same one each time—no matter when I showed up."

The foursome glanced at one another with knowing eyes. They had been right.

"You turned the camera off on your fist visit," Pete said. "Did you have a key to the security cabinet?"

"No, I web-enabled the on-off of the camera system when I installed it. I just never told anyone."

Tom groaned inwardly. That thought had never crossed his technical mind.

"Why didn't you steal all of the artifacts on your first visit?" Pete wondered aloud.

"Guy didn't have a buyer, at least not until he located a crooked dealer in New York City. The dealer found a private collector willing to pay the price. After that, I swiped the artifacts—two at a time—and Davidson shipped them off."

Suzanne asked, "So stealing them all at the same time was never in the cards?"

"Never. After I stole the first two pots, Guy photographed them to prove they were in our possession. Then the dealer went to work. Once the first sale went through, Guy sent me back."

"Philip, that mystified us," Kathy said. "We knew you were on to us because of the bug in the ceiling, but you still kept coming back to the museum. Why?" Despite everything, she felt a little sorry for him.

His eyes smiled. "Oh, you found the bug? I didn't know that. The bug was my idea." He stopped for a few seconds and changed positions. It was obvious the pain had taken its toll. "After the first theft, I never wanted to come back again—not ever. But there wasn't any choice. You see, I'm wanted for burglary in California, and I made the mistake of telling Guy about it. He blackmailed me. 'Do this my way or I'll turn you in,' he said. So I did."

Tom said, "That didn't work out too well."

"That's a fact," Philip said. He stopped and sighed heavily. "I paid a heavy price for Davidson's greed. Plus, bad luck foiled us too—like the night I was forced to smash my way out of the museum. That trapdoor was defective. It closed all by itself, locking me in, and it wasn't the first time."

"It had happened before?"

"Yeah, but I got lucky. It only went down halfway. I squeezed in and got out of there. After the last debacle, I shored the trapdoor up with that piece of two-by-four."

"Good thing it didn't *open* by itself on Roger some night," Kathy half-joked. "It would have flipped the poor man out!"

"I really appreciate you coming to see me," Philip said, holding out his hand. "You saved my life."

They shook hands solemnly and said their goodbyes.

On the way back, Kathy spoke first. "I feel sorry for him."

"Well, he made some bad decisions," Tom said. "He'll have to pay the price."

"It'll be years before he gets out of prison," Suzanne said.

"Oh, well," Pete said flippantly, shrugging his shoulders. "Crime doesn't pay. Never has. What's next?"

GHOSTLY AWARDS

A week later, the Jacksons and Brunellis arrived at the awards ceremony. A chilly wind gusted around them. Dark, ominous-looking clouds whipped overhead across a moonless sky.

Maria looked skyward. "We're in for a downpour."

Yavapai Courthouse Museum was too small for the expected crowd. The executive director of the Opera House, Bob Carlson, had kindly offered the use of its facilities.

"Very generous of him," the Chief said with appreciation.

"Isn't that a little ironic?" Suzanne wondered.

"No kidding," Kathy replied. "Imagine having the awards ceremony where the thieves hung out."

Maria giggled. "I'll miss the ghost. In fact, I'll miss them both. Far more thrilling, even if you don't believe in them. The old Opera House won't ever be the same."

The twins' mother laughed. "This place is more than a century old. It will withstand any old ghost."

When they walked in, the size of the audience stunned the two families. A few dozen people had gathered, and the noise level was high. On the stage up front, dignitaries included Dr. William

Wasson, Bill Holden, Jim Bright, Gloria Waldner, and Mayor Mariana Hernandez.

"It's embarrassing to have to admit that a previous, long-ago mayor and his administration were up to their necks in bootleg whiskey," Kathy said in a hushed voice.

"You won't hear a word about it tonight," Suzanne whispered.

Maria caught the exchange. "You shouldn't talk like that," she hissed, admonishing the two girls. "We have a wonderful mayor today."

"That was a century ago," Sherri reminded them. "There's no comparison."

Someone whispered in the Chief's ear, inviting him on the stage. He declined, choosing to sit with his family and friends.

In the crowd were recognizable faces. Ray Huntley and the technology club team had shown up in force. No one had delivered the news to the club president: the strange spraying sound Pete had heard in the museum entrance was Philip applying a squirt of spray adhesive over the hidden camera's lens. It blurred the images. Quite effectively too.

Charlie Watts had taken the night off to attend the event. Robert Burns sat in the first row, right behind Roger Holloway. Even the Hardiman brothers, Kathy's favorite stagehands, attended.

Television reporters and camera people dotted the back of the hall. Heidi Hoover waved with both arms.

Dean Wasson stood up and adjusted the microphone. The audience settled in expectation.

"Welcome, everyone. Please, make yourself comfortable. As most of you know, I am William Wasson," he said, "the dean of Aztec College and the curator of the Yavapai Courthouse Museum. You all know the story—but it seems a long time ago now, doesn't it?—about how our museum had a ghost running around." There was a murmur of voices.

The dean paused and surveyed the crowd. "Prescott City Police jumped in to help us solve the crime. And, I might add, they performed admirably. Then, a few weeks ago, I called the young

Jackson and Brunelli mystery searchers," he said, peering down at the two families.

At that moment a tremendous crack of lightning stuck nearby. Torrents of rain pounded the building. The Opera House lights flickered as utter silence engulfed the room. The lights hesitated once more before returning to normal.

Charlie Watts yelled, "Maybe he's back!"

The crowd roared with laughter.

"Well," the dean said with a nervous chuckle, "I doubt that, because it turns out we *didn't* have a ghost problem."

"But solving that took the efforts of four fine young people with us here tonight and the extraordinary dedication of one man on this stage, Detective Joe Ryan. With the help of a few others, these folks saved Yavapai Courthouse Museum from an uncertain future."

"The reason we're here," the dean continued, "is to thank those who solved this case. Seeing our two precious Sinagua artifacts arrive back home was one of the greatest days of my life. I'm also told that the FBI has solid leads on the four missing artifacts. We're confident they'll be 'home' in the next few weeks." A standing ovation followed.

"Now," Dean Wasson added, "we've thanked many people for helping solve this case. In addition, we'd like to reward a handful of folks."

"To Roger Holloway, we're awarding a bonus of three thousand dollars. Roger, you stepped up and joined the team. We are most grateful to you. Thank you." More applause.

Tom whispered to the others. "Remember when Detective Ryan told us not to judge a book by its cover?"

"Yes," Suzanne replied. "That was Roger."

"For Prescott's excellent police work, we recognize the superior efforts of Detective Joe Ryan with a ten-thousand-dollar check payable to the Prescott Police Benevolent Association for their important charitable work." The investigator received a standing ovation as he stood.

The four friends held their collective breath.

"And for Tom and Suzanne Jackson and Kathy and Pete Brunelli, for each of the four mystery searchers, we're offering two-years' of all-expenses-paid tuition to Aztec College!"

The crowd stood and cheered as the four friends leaped out of their chairs. After high-fiving each other, they thanked Dean Wasson and shook hands with everyone on the stage. So did their grateful parents. The value of the tuition awards far exceeded $25,000.

An excited Heidi Hoover peeled the foursome away. "Tomorrow's headline is a blockbuster," she shared before rushing off on another assignment. "The truth about the tunnels is on page one. So are you!"

Before the end of the evening, Detective Ryan wandered over to the two families.

"Well," he said, smiling at his band of young detectives, "your impact was huge. I couldn't have done it without you. You made all the difference. And that technology—well, all I can say is, *wow*."

The four mystery searchers grinned and thanked the detective. Tom couldn't have been happier. His father beamed. "We're mighty proud of these young people. Someday they'll make great police officers."

Maria put her arm around her daughter. "Kathy intends to be on Broadway."

"Pete thinks engineering is for him," his father said.

Sherri's eyes flashed. "That leaves our two."

Detective Ryan grinned. Working with the foursome had been a very rewarding experience. He paused for a few seconds and moved closer.

"You know, police work never ends. There's always another mystery in the works," he said, staring at them from behind his thick lenses. "Are you ready?"

EXCERPT FROM BOOK 3

THE SECRETS OF THE MYSTERIOUS MANSION

Chapter 1
The Finding

It was a frigid winter night in the high country of Prescott, Arizona. A dusting of snow, whipped by howling winds, swirled around the Chevy. The reading on the dashboard thermometer continued to drop. Poor driving conditions became worse as the car—buffeted all the way down Route 69—made slow progress. Its windshield wipers beat a rhythmic tune in a vain struggle at visibility.

Heidi Hoover sat in the backseat, peering into the churning darkness, searching for a hidden turnoff. *"There!"* she cried out, pointing through the window on the driver's side. "We almost missed it. There it is."

Tom Jackson—quiet, thoughtful, and steady as a rock—gripped the steering wheel with both hands and cranked a sudden left. The Chevy bumped and bounced over frozen ruts onto a rough dirt road.

"You're sure?" Tom's twin sister, Suzanne, asked. She tightened her front passenger seat belt, staring hard at the bleak scene before her.

Heidi laughed. "Don't worry, Suzie. I drove out here before. Half a mile of this, and then we'll go for a *nice* walk." The way she said it didn't sound nice at all.

Heidi had attended Prescott High, graduating a few years ahead of the twins and their best friends, Kathy and Pete Brunelli. During the time they had all overlapped at school, the four had barely known Heidi. She was a small child—her family refugees from civil war in Mozambique—when they settled in Prescott.

After college, she had landed a job with Prescott's hometown newspaper, *The Daily Pilot*. A short, cute-featured young woman with tight black curls and a dynamic personality, she had soon emerged as the newspaper's star reporter.

Earlier that Thursday evening, Heidi had called Suzanne on her cell phone. "I've got something that's perfect for you guys," she said. "Let's go for a ride—tonight. But make sure you dress for warmth. It's freezing cold out there."

"Tonight?" Suzanne had replied. "It's awfully late. Out where?"

Heidi knew Suzie as a confident, assured person who knew where she was going in life—someone willing to tackle new challenges. Even better, the Jackson twins were half of the four-person mystery searchers team. *"There.* Trust me, the trip will be worthwhile."

The twins would miss having their best friends tag along, but the Brunelli siblings were out of town. The Jacksons and Brunellis had grown up together, and over the years, their families had become exceptionally close. Today, the four were all out from Prescott High for the Christmas break. The Brunellis wouldn't return from an extended gathering of their cousins until the next day—Friday, December twenty-seventh.

"They'll miss out," Tom had said to his sister, lacing up his warm winter boots. The family Christmas tree—harvested from a Prescott forest and still brightly lit—towered above them in the living room.

"Can't help it," Suzanne had said. "Let's go."

The twins picked Heidi up at her apartment on the city's west side. She jumped into the backseat and pointed the way to Route 69.

"Okay, you're being a little mysterious," Suzanne said, turning around in her seat to face Heidi. "Give us a clue."

"We're about to visit a deserted mansion in the forest," Heidi teased. "From a distance."

Suzanne's eyes grew larger. "A *deserted* mansion?"

"From a distance?" Tom asked. "Why not tour the place?"

"You'll soon find out."

The Jackson twins, together with Pete and Kathy, had earned a local reputation for mystery solving. Heidi had covered their two previous cases for the newspaper: the mystery on Apache Canyon Drive, and the ghost in the county courthouse. Both cases had been front-page news—and not just in Prescott.

Along the way, Heidi had become one of the foursome's biggest fans. "You stick to a case like chewing gum," she had once told them. "You never give up. I like that. As a reporter that's just what I do too."

Heidi was also a fan of the twins' father, Edward Jackson—*Chief* Edward Jackson of the Prescott City Police. Most people considered him the most popular chief in the city's history. Heidi agreed. "Fair and honest," she replied whenever anyone asked. "Plus, he knows what he's doing. What's not to like?"

The road was soon close to impassable. Heidi tapped Tom on the shoulder. "Okay, park it. This is the end."

"Here?" Tom asked, slowing to a stop. There was no room to pull over. "In the middle of the road?"

"Uh-huh," Heidi replied. "It's a track, not a road. Believe me, no one's coming behind you. From here, we walk."

Three car doors swung open. The wind whistled through the Chevy, blitzing its occupants with driving snow.

"Whoa, this is *seriously* cold!" Suzanne exclaimed, shivering as she tightened a scarf and zipped up her parka. The twins had both brought thick gloves too. They needed them.

"Told you," Heidi said, chuckling out loud. She buttoned up her big jacket and grabbed her camera bag, leading the way into the night. "You'll warm up soon enough. Follow me."

"How far is the mansion?" Tom shouted into the wind.

"Just two blocks as the crow flies!" Heidi yelled back. "But this crazy path twists and turns on the way there."

Silence descended as the three hikers trekked onward. The rough trail, slippery with fresh-frozen ice under the blowing snow, sloped uphill—so narrow that it allowed passage for only one person at a time. It was slow going.

Tom, breathing hard, drew near to Heidi. "Is this the only way in?"

"Nope, there's a quicker route—an old mining road, but we need to avoid it." She didn't say why, but the county was famous for its gold, silver, copper, lead, and zinc mines—most long abandoned.

Suzanne gazed up into a spectacular night sky to see a million stars twinkling back at her. The biting wind had died away— towering trees provided a degree of shelter—but at ground level it was cold, dark, and dreary. Still, the exertion generated welcome body heat.

Heidi came to a sudden halt and pointed. "Okay, we're going up this hill."

A minute later, they stopped. Long moments passed while the three of them caught their breath. They stood on a hilltop, well above the tree line, gazing at a bleak vista across which eddies of swirling snow ebbed and flowed. Scudding clouds, illuminated fitfully by a waxing moon, raced overhead. Below, a dark forest of stately ponderosa pine circled them, stretching out as far as they could see.

Temperatures continued to drop as the wind kicked up again, hammering the bare, shelter-less hill, gusting in bursts and winding its way down through the sentinel-like trees.

Heidi knelt and opened her camera case. "We're here."

Suzanne locked eyes with her brother. "We don't get it, Heidi. When you say, 'here'..."

Heidi set up a tripod in seconds and attached her camera to it. She stood up. "Look right where I'm pointing. What do you see?"

"Trees!" the twins chorused.

Heidi giggled. "No. Check out the *next* ridge. Notice how the line of trees has a horizontal flat edge running through its center?"

"Oh, wow, yes—I see it now," Suzanne said. "Just faintly."

"Me too," Tom said. "Straight as an arrow."

"Yes, it is. That's the mansion's roofline," Heidi replied. She knelt again to lock the tripod down and focus the camera. She had loaded it with infrared film to capture images in the dark. "Okay, that works. Now relax. Based on my experience over the last two nights, we won't have long to wait."

"Wait for what?" Suzanne asked.

"You'll see."

"You were here the last two nights?" Tom asked incredulously.

"At midnight? *By yourself?*" Suzanne couldn't believe it.

"Yes, and I'll tell you why." The twins crouched down, close on the ground beside Heidi. Suzanne wrapped her arms around her knees for warmth. Long strands of auburn hair blew across her face. She pulled her hood tighter.

"My neighbor is a gold bug—he's panned out here for years. Never laid eyes on the place. Know why? Over time, trees and bushes had surrounded this mansion in the forest—like Sleeping Beauty's castle. It was like, well, *buried*. Last week he stumbled onto it by accident. He walked into a clearing, and there it was." She paused, surveying the scene before them. "He couldn't believe it. Later that night he called me. Next morning, I drove out here. *I couldn't believe it.* You can stand fifty yards away and never see the place."

Heidi stopped again, blowing on her hands for warmth before thrusting them into her pockets. "I scouted around. Bushes had grown across the back door, but someone had cut a narrow channel through them. Not long before, either—the chop marks on the branches were fresh. I knew I wasn't the first person out here."

"Was it locked?" Tom asked.

"Nope. Nor the front door or the garage. They didn't lock a thing."

"Who's 'they'?" Tom asked.

"Keep your eyes on the mansion while we talk," Heidi said. She had an annoying habit of ignoring questions. "You don't want to miss this."

Suzanne asked, "Miss what?"

"After getting in, I toured the place," Heidi continued. "I was careful not to disturb anything—I crept around, quiet like a mouse. But the shots I got with my camera are unbelievable. Someone walked out of there decades ago... *and never returned.* I found a newspaper spread out on the kitchen table. It was from nineteen eighty-nine."

"You mean they left the table behind—their furniture?" Tom asked.

Heidi looked at him for a long moment. He wasn't getting it. "They sure did. And everything else too. And I mean *everything.*" She paused again. "Furniture, silverware, dishes, bedding. Pictures on the walls, family photographs, personal documents, you name it. And that was just the main floor," Heidi continued. "Same story up and down. The place is huge. Creeped me right out."

The twins' minds reeled: a deserted, *abandoned* mansion in the forest. *Why?*

"Weren't you frightened?" Suzanne asked. She couldn't imagine herself walking through a dark, deserted place alone, day or night. Though with Kathy or Pete or her brother—different story...

"Freaked, not frightened," Heidi replied. "But I'll tell you something strange. I *knew* that I wasn't alone. At first, I figured it was my imagination, but I couldn't shake the feeling. It was like a sixth sense."

Suzanne blanched. "Well, that's creepy enough."

"What happened to the people who lived there?" Tom asked.

"That's why you're here," Heidi said, a half smile crossing her face in the dark. "I don't have the answers, but you guys are mystery searchers, and you're good at it. This is big, and it's right up your alley. In fact, my editor thinks this is page-one material. But he wants background. Who were these people? What happened to them? Why did they walk away from everything? And where did they go?"

The trio sat in silence for a couple more minutes, their minds racing.

"Maybe they didn't need this place anymore—" Tom began.

Just then, Heidi stiffened and cried out in a raw whisper. *"There it is!"*

We hope you enjoyed this sneak peak at
The Secrets of the Mysterious Mansion
Pick up your copy at your favorite retailer today!

BIOGRAPHY

Barry Forbes began his writing career in 1980, eventually scripting and producing hundreds of film and video corporate presentations, winning a handful of industry awards along the way. At the same time, he served as an editorial writer for Tribune Newspapers and wrote his first two books, both non-fiction.

In 1997, he founded and served as CEO for Sales Simplicity Software, a market leader which was sold two decades later.

What next? "I always loved mystery stories and one of my favorite places to visit was Prescott, Arizona. It's situated in rugged central Arizona with tremendous locales for mysteries." In 2017, Barry merged his interest in mystery and his skills in writing, adding in a large dollop of technology. The Mystery Searchers Family Book Series was born.

Barry's wife, Linda, passed in 2019 and the series is dedicated to her. "Linda proofed the initial drafts of each book and acted as my chief advisor." The couple had been married for 49 years and had two children. A number of their fifteen grandchildren provided feedback on each book.

Contact Barry: barry@mysterysearchers.com

ALSO BY BARRY FORBES

The Mystery Searchers Family Book Series

BOOK 1: THE MYSTERY ON APACHE CANYON DRIVE

A small child wanders out onto a busy Arizona highway! In a hair-raising
rescue, sixteen-year-old twins Tom and Suzanne Jackson save the little girl
from almost certain death. Soon, the brother-and-sister team up with their
best friends, Kathy and Pete Brunelli, on a perilous search for the child's
mother—and her past. The mystery deepens as one case becomes two,
forcing the four friends to deploy concealed technological tools along
Apache Canyon Drive. The danger level ramps up with the action, and the
"mystery searchers" are born.

BOOK 2: THE GHOST IN THE COUNTY COURTHOUSE

A mysterious "ghost" bypasses the security system of the Yavapai
Courthouse Museum and makes off with four of the museum's most
precious Native American relics. At the invitation of the museum's curator,
Dr. William Wasson, the mystery searchers jump onto the case and deploy a
range of technological devices to discover the ghost's secrets. If the ghost
strikes again, the museum's very future is in doubt. A dangerous game of
cat and mouse ensues.

BOOK 3: THE SECRETS OF THE MYSTERIOUS MANSION

Heidi Hoover, a good friend and a top reporter for Prescott's newspaper,
The Daily Pilot, introduces the mystery searchers to a mysterious mansion
in the forest—at midnight! The mansion is under siege from unknown
"hunters." *Who are they? What are they searching for?* Good old-fashioned
detective work and a couple of technological tricks ultimately reveal the
truth. A desperate race ensues, but time is running out . . .

BOOK 4: THE HOUSE ON CEMETERY HILL

There's a dead man walking, and it's up to the mystery searchers to figure out why. That's the challenge set by Mrs. Leslie McPherson, a successful but eccentric Prescott businesswoman. The mystery searchers team up with their favorite detective and use technology to spy on high-tech criminals at Cemetery Hill. It's a perilous game with heart-stopping moments of danger.

BOOK 5: THE TREASURE OF SKULL VALLEY

Suzanne discovers a map hidden in the pages of a classic old book at the thrift store where she works. It's titled "My Treasure Map" and leads past Skull Valley, twenty miles west of Prescott, and into the high-desert country—to an unexpected, shocking, and elusive treasure. "Please help," the note begs. The mystery searchers utilize the power and reach of the internet to trace the movement of people and events . . . half a century earlier.

BOOK 6: THE VANISHING IN DECEPTION GAP

A text message to Kathy sets off a race into the unknown. "There are pirates operating out here and they're dangerous. I can't prove it but I need your help." Who sent the message? Out where? Pirates—on land! How weird is that? The mystery searchers dive in, but it might be too late. Whoever sent the message has vanished into thin air.

BOOK 7: THE GETAWAY LOST IN TIME

A stray dog saves the twins from a dangerous predator on the hiking trail at Watson Lake. In a surprising twist, the dog leads the mystery searchers to the recent suspicious death of an elderly recluse with a mysterious past. The four young sleuths join the Sheriff's Office of Yavapai County and Heidi Hoover, the star reporter of *The Daily Pilot*, in the search for the heartless perpetrator who caused her death.

BOOK 8: THE HUNT FOR THE ELUSIVE MASTERMIND

The mystery searchers embark on one of their strangest cases—the kidnapping of the wife of one of the city's most prominent bankers. The mystery deepens as the baffling questions emerge: Who are the kidnappers —beneath their disguises? What happened to the ransom money? It soon becomes clear that the hostage may not be the only one in danger . . .

BOOK 9: THE LEGEND OF RATTLER MINE

In a rocky ravine north of the Flying W Dude Ranch, the mystery searchers save an unconscious man from certain death. Little do they know that they're about to step into a century-old legend that's far more dangerous than it first appears. Does Rattler Mine really exist? If it does, exactly where is it? And who is the mysterious man—or woman—willing to risk everything for it . . . *no matter the cost?*

BOOK 10: THE HAUNTING OF WAINRICH MANOR

It's the Chief's birthday party, and the Jackson and Brunelli families gather to celebrate at his favorite restaurant. Little do they know that they are about to cross paths with the charming Mrs. Roberta Robertson, who will introduce the mystery searchers to a bizarre case. Someone is haunting One Wainrich Manor, a mansion abandoned for sixty years. *Who and why?*

BOOK 11: THE DAYLIGHT HEIST ON WHISKEY ROW (COMING SUMMER, 2022)

A daring daylight heist takes place along Prescott's Whiskey Row during the annual Frontier Days parade. Detective Joe Ryan believes the million-dollar robbery is a professional hit, executed by out-of-town criminals. *But is it?* The mystery searchers take on one of their most puzzling cases yet.